Shadow of
a Stranger

**Center Point
Large Print**

**This Large Print Book carries the
Seal of Approval of N.A.V.H.**

ॐ श्री गणेशाय नमः

Shadow of a Stranger

Anne Maybury

Center Point Publishing
Thorndike, Maine

ISBN: 1-58547-019-8

Library of Congress Cataloging-in-Publication Data

Maybury, Anne.
    Shadow of a stranger / Anne Maybury.
      p. cm.
    ISBN 1-58547-019-8 (lib. bdg. : alk. paper)
    1. Large type books. I. Title.

PR6025.A943 S52 2000
823'.914—dc21

                                                    99-056103

I

THIS WAS A MOMENT when she should have known absolute happiness. She was in a new country and a new adventure was beginning. Out of the window of the train rolling north from New York to Toronto was the stretched blue silk of the sky under a world of unbroken snow.

A new world for Tess Bellairs!

And yet the excitement of it all was tempered with her own deep personal problem. Her mind had only one thought: *Perhaps this visit to Toronto will save my marriage;* her heart held only one emotion: *Oh, Johnnie! Johnnie! We* did *love one another, didn't we? We do!* She clung to that. *We* do *love one another—*

It was said, wasn't it, that the first year of marriage is always the most difficult because of the adjustments which have to be made. Tess had gone with winged feet to her wed-

5

ding; had said with conviction and glorious faith in herself and Johnnie—that she would love and cherish him forever. And yet, only a few months later. . . . *Stop! If there is disillusion, perhaps Johnnie feels it, too! Perhaps he thinks you haven't come up to his high dreams, either!*

She heard the lonely wolf-howl of the train and felt the drag of brakes as it slowed down at a level crossing. She tried to fling herself into the excitement of it all. The future was rosy and it was up to her to see that it stayed so. She opened her overnight case to get out a new packet of cigarettes and the mirrored lid gave her back her reflection. She had taken off her hat and her chestnut hair was only a little ruffled. Her gray eyes were unexpectedly bright, she thought with amusement, after the late nights she had had at the Burnses' hospitable house. The lines of her face were clearcut—small straight nose; firm chin, wide mouth curved upwards at the corners. She wore a coat of sapphire blue, Johnnie's favorite color, with a collar of rich dark otter. Under it, her suit was a shade lighter and she wore two rows of river pearls.

"You'll do!" she told herself and snapped the lid of the case down and lit her cigarette.

The train gained speed again. Tess slid out of her coat, tossed it over the back of her seat and sat cradling herself in the comfort of the deep chair in the lounge-parlor car. She had just ordered coffee and she sat staring out of the window, waiting for it. There was so much to see, so much that was new and strange; yet her thoughts crept back once more to Johnnie. She seemed to see his face superimposed over the landscape, fair, narrow, laughing, every feature faintly tilted like the pagan Pan: light eyes, pointed chin. He was charming and high-spirited and popular wherever he went. But those very things that had enchanted her were proving to be the ones that were shaking the foundations of her marriage. Johnnie loved parties and fun. He had a clever, inventive brain but he lacked the stability to keep him in a job; he grew bored with routine. Tess had told herself: "He'll change. He'll grow up." Perhaps she would already see a change in him after the two months he had been out here.

She remembered that day, early in December, when he had told her about the letter from Toronto. For some weeks before she learned of it, Johnnie had been behaving with a kind of secret excitement that had at the time puzzled and alarmed her.

Experience during their months of marriage had taught her a wry lesson regarding this unpredictable husband of hers, so that she kept asking herself, "What is he up to *this* time?" and then, one evening, he told her all about it.

Relief that it was good news and not bad had had an odd reaction. She was angry. She had had weeks of unnecessary anxiety.

"You might have *told* me!" she cried. "It was mean to keep it to yourself and let me wonder what it was all about!"

But Johnnie had merely laughed.

"I didn't want to tell you until I'd decided. I wanted no persuasion—it was something I had to make up my own mind about. After all, Uncle Luke had ignored me all my life, he never even sent me a birthday or Christmas present, so my first reaction was to resent being summoned, like some poor relative running for crumbs! Just because my Aunt Stacey had died, Uncle Luke decided to take notice of me out of loneliness or boredom!"

That Johnnie had a rich uncle was a complete surprise to Tess. He had never mentioned his father's cousin—but now she saw that long ago he had given up hope of any contact with him and had therefore shut him out of his thoughts.

Johnnie told her now about Uncle Luke Bellairs, how he had risen, by brain and dynamic force, from nothing to become a very rich man.

"Now that my aunt is dead, I suppose he's got a lot of money to leave to his near relatives. That"—Johnnie had leaned over the back of Tess' chair and dropped a kiss on top of her head—"is why I'm accepting that invitation to visit him. He must be quite seventy and somebody's got to inherit! I can pocket a devil of a lot of pride for half a million dollars!"

Old Luke Bellairs had asked him out for a minimum stay of two months. Now that his mind was made up, Johnnie gleefully threw up his job with the estate agents, cashed the thousand-dollar check his uncle had sent him and booked his airline ticket.

Then, a few weeks ago a letter had arrived telling Tess to come out and join him. Ample money was sent for her fare and expenses.

"Sub-let the flat, if you can, for an indefinite period. If you can't, just shut it up; buy yourself some pretty clothes and be prepared to charm Uncle Luke. He likes me, but I've a feeling that whether he also likes my wife is going to play a very important part in what Charles Dickens called our 'great expectations'!"

So, Tess had sub-let the flat in Bayswater, and after a tedious filling-in of forms had managed to get a United States permit to visit her old school-friend Sally Burns who was now married to an American newspaperman living in Connecticut.

Tess had enjoyed every moment of her stay with the young Burns family at Sarraway Fields and nothing dimmed her horizon. She was going to join Johnnie and he seemed to have settled down very happily in the big house in Toronto.

The steward set her coffee down on the little low table. Tess paid for it and as she turned to stir in sugar, the magazine on her lap slid to the floor. Reaching to pick it up, her shoulder jolted against something that held, firm and hard.

Someone, towering above her, called out a laughing warning.

"Hey!"

There was a sharp clink of ice against glass.

She hit against a man's arm and she jerked back, looking up.

Vivid blue eyes, the kind one saw in the faces of Nordic men, met hers.

"I'm so sorry," Tess said quickly. "I didn't know anyone was near me. Have I spilt your drink?"

"No." The man edged himself into the chair next to her. "Anyway, it wasn't your fault. The train lurched and my balance was never my strong point!"

His face itself wasn't familiar to her; but somewhere recently she had looked across a space and seen the steady scrutiny of just such intense blue eyes. Somewhere . . . Where?

And then she remembered. In the vast, bustling hall of Grand Central Station in New York, while Sally was making Tess promise to come and see them again before she returned to England, Bill Burns had turned to a little group standing near them and had hailed someone. And during the excited greeting of friends meeting unexpectedly, deep blue eyes had looked across at Tess and smiled.

She hadn't known his name. He was just a friend whom Sally and Bill's friends were seeing off. People jostled past them, laughed, shouted at one another, ran for trains and Sally's bright eyes, darting from Tess to the unknown man, mirrored her silent message to these unexpectedly met friends. "Come on, introduce us. This could be a traveling companion for Tess." She had even begun to say: "If your friend is also traveling to Toronto—" when the man looked at his watch and turned away, saying, "It's just five minutes to nine. This is where I hustle my red-cap wherever he is!" He shot a smile at them all and the moment for an introduction was gone.

"You know," said the man, setting down his

drink, we met at Grand Central Station, didn't we? I heard you speak and I thought, 'She's English.' "

"You know Sally and Bill Burns?"

"I was being seen off by some friends who knew them." He looked at Tess with interest. "Do you live in Toronto?"

She shook her head. "I'm joining my husband there. He's staying with his uncle. You're Canadian, aren't you?"

"From Vancouver. I'm staying in Toronto for some time, too."

Tess liked what she saw of him. He would be about thirty, and there was a suggestion of a deep inner strength. His hair was the kind that would have curled had he let it; it swept back crisply from his wide forehead; his mouth was kind and grave above his firm chin. But the eyes drew her again.

"Smoke?" he was asking, watching her.

"I've just put one out."

"But this is an occasion. Our second meeting!" He was smiling. "I think the old tradition of the Red Indians was that you smoked a pipe of peace when you met."

"Put like that," she said lightly, "how can I refuse?"

"Are you settling in Toronto?" He lit the long American cigarette she had chosen.

"I shouldn't think so. I don't know very much about what's happening until I meet Johnnie, my husband—" She paused, and then, because she found it easy to talk to him she explained, "My husband has been out here for two months, and he sent for me to join him."

"And this is your first glimpse of Canada?"

"Yes." She glanced sideways at him. "Are you on your way back to Vancouver?"

"Eventually. I'm footloose at the moment. I've been traveling around the world—'east of the sun and west of the moon.' And now I'm spending a few weeks on what we call the Eastern seaboard before making that long journey home."

"How lovely to have traveled like that!"

He blew smoke towards the window. "I've had wanderlust all my life, with no means of indulging it. Then suddenly the opportunity came and I seized it. I've been all over the place and you'd better be careful because I can be a bore talking about it! People aren't really interested, you know, in places they're never likely to see—"

"Oh, but I am! It's the next best thing to going! If someone talks interestingly you feel you've been there too!"

He glanced at her, eyebrows raised, and then

lifted his glass with a small, toasting gesture.

"Sometimes," he said, "I drink to some of the most memorable things I've seen and say to them: 'I'll be seeing you again.' And I hope I will. I've walked in the ornamental gardens of the Taj Mahal in moonlight; I've stood in front of the Sphinx and wondered if it's really true that under the layers of two thousand years or more of dust, it has a ring of amber around its neck; I've walked in the Forbidden City of Peking and seen the scarlet and gold temples—" he broke off. "You mustn't encourage me by looking so interested! You see, Mrs.—" He hesitated. "I'm sorry, Grand Central is the place for farewells, not introductions, so no one told me who you were."

"I'm Tess Bellairs."

"And I'm Angus Dalzell—prefix 'Doctor.'"

Their eyes held with friendly enjoyment.

"Thirteen hours is a long time to travel alone," said Angus Dalzell. "Will you lunch with me?"

"Thank you. I'd like to."

Over lunch, it was Tess who did the talking. She found herself telling this young doctor that her parents were dead, sliding away from the memory of the car crash that had flung her to safety and orphaned her in one dreadful night on the Great West Road. She

14

told him that before her marriage she had been assistant secretary to a fiery and fanatical member of Parliament who had expected his staff to burn with the same zeal over the Party as he. "And now I'm going to stay with my husband's uncle, Luke Bellairs."

"You said Luke Bellairs?"

"Yes," she said, surprised at his surprise. "Why, do you know him?"

"Good heavens, no! I don't mix in those circles! But I know *of* him! Everyone in Canada knows that name!"

"I believe he started his life as a gold prospector."

"He did," Angus Dalzell agreed, "and now he has mining interests, he dabbles in steel, he owns housing estates. But for all that, he hasn't built himself a palace! I believe he lives very well, but quite simply."

"So I won't have to eat off a gold plate," she laughed.

"Not quite. But you'll have to be prepared, since you're related to him, to feature largely in the gossip columns of the newspapers; to be noticed wherever you go—"

"*Me?*" she cried in alarm. "But I'm nobody! I'm not 'society.' "

"That doesn't matter. Anyone concerned with your uncle is 'news' all across Canada.

You can't escape, Mrs. Bellairs!"

The laughter had gone out of his face and something in his gaze startled and dismayed her. A flash of pity, a mysterious shadow of compassion? Pity? Compassion? *"You can't escape, Mrs. Bellairs—"*

And then the look vanished. Angus Dalzell began to talk about Vancouver, telling her that sometime during her stay in Canada, she must see the West. It would be easy since her husband's uncle had business connections there, too. She must get him to take her.

Yet, while they continued to talk, while he insisted that she must taste some Oka cheese made by the monks in the monastery near Montreal, the feather of premonition which had touched her would not be shaken off. Absurd, she told herself, to read significant meaning in those five words! All he had meant was, "You can't escape being a 'somebody' if you have Luke Bellairs for an uncle."

And yet the memory of that involuntary look of swift compassion that had crossed his face lingered and troubled her with its hint of a secret meaning to his words—

He had changed the conversation, telling her about himself. A serious illness had forced him to give up his work at a Vancouver hospital and when he was better he was told to take a long holiday.

"But I'm not the kind to idle my life away." He was leaning back in his chair, staring at the snow-white landscape. "So I got myself various jobs as ship's doctor. I was lucky, there were three temporary vacancies and that's how I managed to see something of the world."

He was, Tess found, a man as capable of silence as of speech. He did not weary her during that journey by talking all the time. He sat for long periods quite quietly in the chair next to hers and stared out of the window or read his paper. Yet there was as much companionship in his quiet as in his conversation. She had only once before in her life known anyone who could make silences so easy, and that was her father. Watching the sky darken and the snow begin to fall lightly as birds' feathers on that wide winter land she realized that she could now remember her father and mother without the shuddering horror that had clung to her mind for months after the accident.

When Johnnie had come into her life, it had been like blinding sunlight after four months of numbness and shock. Between that night in January when the car had skidded on an icy patch on the road and crashed into a wall, and the evening of the party where she had met Johnnie, there had been a kind of twilight across her life.

Tess had escaped with merely bruises and cuts to her body, but such shock to her mind that for some time afterwards she had had black-outs that terrified her. "What do I *do* during those times?" she had demanded of the doctors. They had assured her that she had done nothing out of the ordinary. Time would heal, they said, and suggested a whole heap of impossible ways to hasten that healing. "Go for a cruise," they said. "Take yourself off to North Africa or the Bahamas and lie in the sun and meet new people and dance and enjoy yourself!" As though a girl of twenty-four, the daughter of charming but improvident parents, could spend a few hundred pounds with as little consideration as she would give to putting a sixpence in a slot machine for a railway ticket!

She had recuperated for a while in a place in North Devon and then returned to work. But her final emergence came on that evening when she had met Johnnie at a cocktail party and halfway through it, he had said:

"Look, this is a dud party! Let's escape. I've got a beautiful new car and I want to show it off to someone! It's a lovely night—let's go and find a place in the country and have dinner."

Slowly the veils of shock dropped from her

as day after day Johnnie took her dining or driving or dancing. He "magicked" her by his irresponsible gaiety; he could turn on charm like a tap of sparkling water, and that was the quality which got him his jobs too easily—far too easily! The trouble was that, intelligent though he was, he had no staying power. He had helped a friend run a garage; had had two jobs in the city and had worked in a West-end estate agents. Nobody sacked him; he just walked out of each one because he was bored.

But whatever Johnnie was like, she would always be grateful that he had cured her of that horror of blackouts. She could remember now with a kind of impartial pity towards herself, how she had asked the Scots doctor, "Is my brain affected? Please tell me—" His reassurance should have convinced her, but it hadn't. "You're as sane as any of us, stop asking nonsensical questions, girl!"

When she knew that she was well again, she had told Johnnie about it.

"You look fine to me, sweet," he had said and held her close and kissed her. "Maybe those doctors didn't suggest the right cure! They should have said: 'Go out and get yourself someone to love.' And you do, don't you, Tess?"

"I do. Oh, darling, I do!"

Love and laughter had been the right medicine. The old adage of Omar Khayyám,

"Unborn to-morrow and dead yesterday,
Why fret about them if to-day be sweet?"

was Johnnie's philosophy—

It was nearly ten o'clock when the Toronto-bound train reached Union Station.

"Someone will be meeting you, of course—" Angus began.

"Johnnie will."

The train pulled to a stop and he held out his hand.

"Thank you for making my journey so enjoyable."

Tess wanted to say, "Perhaps we'll meet again." But their acquaintanceship was so transient that common sense told her they would never meet again—

They smiled at one another. All her life, whenever she saw a deeply blue-eyed man, she would think of Doctor Angus Dalzell!

"Good-bye . . ."

"Good-bye! . . ."

The red-cap collected her luggage and took her down the long platform and through the barrier to the station hall.

Eagerly Tess looked among the crowd. Johnnie wasn't there. She supposed he would be outside with a car or a taxi. The porter wheeled her luggage out. A flurry of snow spattered her. She felt the tiny flakes on her eyelids and blinked them away, looking for Johnnie.

People jostled her; people met, embraced, laughed, climbed into taxis and drove away.

Still, she could not see Johnnie.

A feeling of alarm ran through her. It was perfectly easy, of course, to dive into a taxi and go to Uncle Luke Bellairs' home. But when you arrive in a city for the first time, there is a kind of alarming emptiness about not being met.

"Can't you find your husband?"

She whirled around and saw Angus coming up behind her.

"I can't think what's happened! He should be here." The snow felt icy against her face. "Perhaps it's just that he's late."

"Or has made a mistake about the date or time of your arrival."

"Oh, no. I told him which train I'd be catching and he said he'd meet me."

"I'm getting a taxi. Let me take you where you want to go."

"But suppose Johnnie arrives in the meantime?"

"Well, if he does, he'll be very late. The train has been in over ten minutes and you're

21

shivering."

She was. She felt shriveled inside her beautiful new coat with the dark otter collar.

"If your husband comes, he'll guess what has happened. Please let me take you where you want to go. You can't hang around here in this wind."

"Thank you," she cried, trying not to let her teeth chatter.

Angus Dalzell was giving instructions to her impatient red-cap. Luggage was piled into the taxi and she gave him the address.

"It's uptown," Angus said, "in a fine district just off St. Clair Avenue."

He might have said "First turning to the left beyond the Taj Mahal" for all it meant to her. She was cold and dispirited and vaguely frightened.

Inside the taxi Angus persuaded her to smoke.

"It'll do you good," he said. "I'd like to stop at the hotel and give you something good and strong to warm you up, but I guess you'd rather go straight home."

The taxi passed the tall skyscraper buildings on University Avenue where every tree branch was outlined in snow gleaming in the strong lights.

II

TESS WAS grateful to Angus that he didn't try to make conversation. He let her sit quietly in her corner of the taxi, trying to argue to herself that Johnnie had merely been late; that he had got caught up in a traffic jam; that he was ill.

In that grateful quiet speeding through the Toronto streets, she sought for plausible reasons for Johnnie's nonarrival.

The taxi turned into a wide road of large houses standing in their own grounds. The smooth whiteness of the snow and the lamplight and the golden squares of the lighted windows gave a Christmas card effect. They turned into a drive and Tess peered out of the window.

"You're home now," Angus said, "and you'll soon be warm and welcome," but his voice faded and she knew why.

The great house stood in pitch darkness.

Even the light over the porch was out and every uncurtained window showed the same vacant look.

Tess climbed out of the taxi and stood with Angus, staring at the forbidding façade. The taxi driver was carrying her luggage to the porch and dumping it there.

Angus looked at her anxiously. "I don't quite know what to do. I think I'd better wait till the door opens."

"Please don't. There must be someone in! They're probably at the back of the house. At any rate, I'm home—and thank you for everything. You've been so kind."

"If I knew you better I'd insist on waiting with you. As it is, I suppose I'm a stranger and must do as I'm told!"

"I really *am* all right now," she assured him.

He smiled—doubtfully, gave her a light salute and got back into the taxi. Tess pressed the bell at the side of the heavy door, half turning to watch the rear light of the taxi disappear.

There was no sound inside the house. She waited and then rang again. No light went on in that gaping blackness; no movement was made in that silence; no sound came save the distant roar of traffic on the sludgy roads.

Tess stepped back from the great covered porch and looked up at the dark house. Immediately she darted aside in alarm. Right over the doorway hung a gigantic icicle. At any moment, she thought, that vicious thing could fall, like a silver spear whose thrust could kill.

Imagination played tricks. She saw it as an ill omen and the next moment pulled herself together. There were probably millions of icicles in this city on such a freezing night.

She went down the porch steps and around the house to look for lights in the back rooms. She almost ran along the narrow, slippery path and as she turned the second corner, the moon swam clear of clouds and flooded the building and the garden. As a contrast to the silver sky, blankness and darkness stared at her from the house.

Tess reached out a hesitant hand and turned the handle of the back door. It opened. She told herself there was nothing to fear; this was the house where Johnnie lived. . . . She took a deep breath and walked into the blackness beyond the pool of light the moon made.

She found herself standing in a small hallway. Feeling along the wall, her fingers found a light switch and flicked it on. Rich, glowing color sprang into view through a glass door on her left. Cushions and carpet and chairs, red and yellow-green, should have given her a sense of comfort that there was, after all, gaiety in this blank house. Instead they only accentuated the emptiness. Ahead of her was another door. She opened it and found herself looking into the clinical whiteness of a kitchen.

Tess took a few steps over the threshold, switched on another light and stood looking around. Sink and stove, pots and pans were spotless. There was neither smell of latent cooking nor warmth from the stove, just coolness and silence.

But there wasn't silence!

She stood immovable, holding her breath, and heard a small sound from somewhere on the floor above her; a stir, a movement and then a clearer sound like creeping footsteps—

She could hold her breath no longer. She let it out slowly and then listened again.

The sound seemed a little nearer. It could, of course, be a tree outside, shaken by the wind. But there *was* no wind. Someone in another house—but the next house was a long way away.

A nameless fear seized her. Her instinct was to run out again into the street, to escape something that lived and breathed so horribly near her—and did not want to be seen.

And then, once more, she told herself. "But

Johnnie lives here! There's nothing to fear!"

She called out.

"Is anybody there?"

There was no answer. For a moment the sound ceased. Then, somewhere above her, it began again.

"It's Tess here—" her voice sounded thin and high. She stood for a moment frozen with fear, hearing another sound, a muffled dragging noise which seemed now to come from the ground floor. Whoever was in the house was nearer now. Too near!

Suddenly Tess unfroze and her limbs moved again. She turned and fled out into the garden. She rushed around the house and halfway along the path that led to the front drive, she ran full tilt into a tall, dark man.

She gave a small, startled scream.

Arms reached out and gripped her.

"Canada isn't yet old enough to have its ghosts!" said a laughing voice. "Don't be afraid."

It was Angus.

"I thought you'd gone. I thought—" Her teeth chattered. "I thought I was utterly alone—except for—"

"For what?"

His steady hands holding her gave her back her strength and she looked up at him.

"Why did you come back?"

"I had an uncomfortable feeling that I shouldn't have left you at the door of a dark house, I should have waited for someone to come and let you in. Or at least, for a light to show. So, I came back just to assure myself that you were inside and warm and with your people."

"I don't know where Johnnie is—"

"You must have been expected on some other day. That must be the simple explanation—"

Simple!

She *had* to tell him, to trust him, though he was a stranger.

"Something odd is going on in the house!" she began and told him what she had heard.

He took her arm and led her around to the back door. As they turned the corner, moonlight shone on to a built-out studio.

Tess gave a little cry. "Look—oh *look!*"

Sightless eyes stared from an ivory pale face. There was no body; just a face and blackness around it.

Angus followed her gaze and then crossed the paved patio and peered through the window.

"It's somebody's studio and what you see is an unfinished mask—at least I'll guess it's unfinished. Don't be afraid. It's hanging on a black screen, that's why it looks so eerie!"

He walked into the kitchen and Tess followed.

"You stay here, I'm going to look around."

"I think I'd rather come with you. I'd feel safer!"

They went through a green baize door and into a great square hall. A staircase rose, curving upwards. On a long, cherry-wood table stood a lamp and two poinsettias, their flowers like red stars. Angus opened doors leading out of the hall switching on lights so that the whole ground floor of the house blazed.

"The sound," Tess said, following him into a room, "seemed to come first from upstairs and then—" She stopped dead. "That window!"

"They've left it open. Why?" He turned questioningly.

"But it *wasn't* open when I arrived!" She had joined him at the window. "You see, it looks on to the porch and I looked at the windows as I stood waiting for someone to answer the doorbell and they were all tightly closed. That's the sound I heard, someone opening this window!"

"I think," Angus said gravely, "you disturbed a burglar, and he escaped this way." He reached up, with his gloved hands and closed it again. Then he regarded Tess. "Look, it's far too late for you to be hanging around an empty house. I'll get you a room for the night at my hotel, it's only around the corner, and you can come along here in the morning."

"Thank you, Dr. Dalzell, but I'd better leave a note, hadn't I, to say that I've arrived and where I am?"

"I think, too, you'd better save your energy and just call me Angus."

"Angus, then," she said without question, vaguely grateful for the friendliness. "Nothing seems to be touched here, but it *must* have been a burglar, mustn't it?"

"Well, I can't imagine anyone who lives here behaving in that odd way! You don't creep about your own house!"

"Had we better tell the police?"

"I think we ought to wait and tell your uncle and your husband first." He laid a hand on her arm. "Come along, Tess, I'm taking you out of here—" He stopped suddenly and listened.

Footsteps were mounting the steps of the porch. There were voices, and a key clattered in the door.

"What in the name of blazes does this mean?" bellowed a voice. "All these durned lights on?"

And suddenly the doorway was filled with a

broad giant of a man with thick white hair standing out like a brush around his head. Sharp eyes looked from Angus to Tess.

"What's the meaning of this?"

Behind the man, a girl and an old woman were taking off their overshoes, tossing them down and coming quickly to join the big man. Then, behind them all, Tess saw Johnnie.

He pushed forward into the room.

"For Pete's sake! Tess! When did you get here?"

"It seems hours ago!"

"But you weren't expected until the eighteenth!"

"I said the sixteenth in my letter."

"Johnnie's wife!" cried the big man and hurled his coat on to a chair, coming forward to take her hand. "So that's who you are! Great snakes, girl! You come all this way and there's no one to meet you!" he looked at Angus.

"This," Tess said, "is Dr. Angus Dalzell. He very kindly waited to see that I was all right. He's a friend of some friends of mine in Sarraway Fields. I met him on the train and when Johnnie wasn't at the station to meet me, he brought me here in his taxi."

"Nice of you," said Johnnie shortly.

"And by the way," Tess went on, "I think you should know that a—"

"Take your coat off, girl! Sit down; sit down both of you. We'll all have a drink and—"

"Uncle Luke, I think you'd better know—"

"I'll know everything when we're all comfortable," he interrupted her. "You're shivering! Don't wonder at it—it's no night to stand ringing at doorbells that don't get answered. Johnnie, get the drinks, and be quick." He turned and nodded towards the old woman who walked with slightly bent back, towards the central heating thermostat, turning it up, complaining, "It's cold in here!"

"This is my sister, Johnnie's aunt, Ginevra."

"Welcome," said a slightly rasping voice.

Ginevra Bellairs was small and thin with a pointed face and green eyes. She might have been sixty, she might have been eighty. With garish makeup and old clothes, she could have impersonated one of Macbeth's witches. As it was, she wore a wild-mink coat and diamonds on her long, skinny fingers. Her eyes had an uncomfortable, piercing quality.

"And this is my niece, Johnnie's cousin, Olivia."

There was no reason for that wave of antagonism Tess felt reaching out to her from the girl who took her hand with cool reluctance. Tess smiled, ready for friendship, ready to like—but the eyes that met hers held no warmth.

Raven-black hair swept back in two gleaming wings from an oval face; flecks of gold shone in the light eyes. Olivia had just thrown off a coat of silky beaver to reveal a simple and dramatic red dress. If Aunt Ginevra Bellairs could have been one of Macbeth's witches, Olivia could as easily have impersonated a young Lady Macbeth—

Tess looked across at Angus and knew that he was waiting, just as she was, to get a word in about the intruder in the house.

Luke, still talking, strode over to the tray of drinks Johnnie had brought in, saying:

"You'll have a drink, Dalzell. Where're you from?"

"Vancouver."

"Fine city. I know it well. Johnnie, you'd better go and fetch that letter of Tess', just to see who made the mistake in the date."

"I didn't," he said crossly, "but I'll get it in a minute."

"We've all been over at the Club," old Luke said. "I was playing in a curling match and the family came to watch. It's very seldom that the house is left entirely empty, in fact I can't remember it happening. Ginevra's usually in, or I am and I'm sorry it should have been this evening. How did you get in?"

"That's what I want to tell you about, Uncle

33

Luke. The back door was open, and—"

"You said you'd locked it," he interrupted, swinging around on Ginevra.

"Oh but I did."

"Mrs. Bellairs," Angus said firmly, "Tess is trying to tell you that she heard—"

When old Luke Bellairs wanted to speak he could shout everyone down. He was glaring at Ginevra.

"If you'd locked the back door Tess couldn't have got in. I'm glad she did, but what in the world came over you, leaving the house open for burglars?"

"Aunt Ginevra *did* lock it, you know," Olivia put in coolly. "I was in the sun-room and I saw her." She took a tall glass from Johnnie, smiling up at him. The smile did nothing, though, to soften her face!

"Mr. Bellairs," Angus' voice had risen. He could command a hearing, too. "When Tess opened the back door she was certain she heard someone in the house. She was scared. Fortunately I didn't like to leave her standing ringing the bell of an empty house and I came back to see if she was all right. We entered the house together and found"—he pointed—"that window open."

"The devil it was!" Luke shot up from his chair, brushed past Johnnie who held his

34

drink out for him and strode out of the room.

Ginevra looked about her. "Nothing seems to be missing, here, but Luke's safe is in his bedroom."

They could hear the old man tramping overhead.

"He keeps a lot of rare things in his bedroom and his study," Ginevra explained, swinging her glass gently so that the ice tinkled. "I always tell him that he should have his treasures in here, on show for his friends to see. But he says he bought them for his own pleasure and he likes to see them around him when he wakes and when he works."

Johnnie had finished handing around the drinks and came and sat down by Tess' side on the settee.

They were silent for minutes listening. Then heavy footsteps thumped down the stairs, the door next to the living-room opened.

"That's Luke's study," said Ginevra. "He'll be making sure the vase is safe."

"The vase?"

Johnnie said laughing, "Oh, you'll be shown it soon enough! It's a *famille noire;* very, very rare and valuable. It doesn't appeal to me artistically, and I suspect it doesn't to Uncle Luke either!"

"It's worth thousands of dollars, though!"

Olivia said sleepily; "thousands of lovely dollars!"

Johnnie's arm slid along the back of the settee, his fingers played a light affectionate tattoo on Tess' shoulder. Olivia watched them both; her eyes had the hypnotic golden stare of a cat.

"Of course," Johnnie went on as no one spoke, "Uncle Luke deserves to be burgled, insisting on always turning out lights. He could have the whole place floodlit and it wouldn't make a hole in his bank balance!"

Tess looked around the room. It was tastefully furnished with well-polished pieces of old maple and cherry-wood furniture. There were bright chintzes, ruby red on a white ground; green cushions and a lot of flowers, beautifully arranged. It was very much a room made comfortable by women—first by Luke's wife, and then by Ginevra.

The old man came thumping back, filling the room again with his body and his personality.

"Everything's intact so I won't ring the police, but I'll call in tomorrow and tell them." He looked about him. "Where's my drink?"

"At your elbow," Ginevra told him.

Angus set down his glass and rose saying he must go.

"Thanks for looking after Tess," Luke said.

"You going to be in Toronto long?"

"A few weeks."

"Work?"

"No, idling. I'm on my way home after wandering around the world."

"You've been East?" Interest flared in the old man's eyes.

"Yes, Japan, China, India—"

"So have I, son. So have I. This is great! So few people here in Toronto know those parts. They go to Europe and think they've seen the world. When I was young, I went everywhere, took any sort of job from cabin boy to dock laborer. I went again about fifteen years ago with money to burn this time. But you've been more recently and I'd like to talk about it; I'd like to know what's changed; what you saw—"

"I should think almost everything has changed," Angus said wryly, "except those ageless things like the Taj Mahal and the Forbidden City—"

"You come around tomorrow night and let's talk. Come to dinner. Can you?"

"Thank you, sir."

"And I'll show you my library. I've got a very fine collection of travel books, hundreds of them, old and new—some first editions. I'd like you to see them."

"I'll be in my element," Angus said with a

smile, held out his hand, and took his leave.

The old man sat, one white eyebrow raised quizzically and watched Angus go through the door with Johnnie.

"Well, girl, tell me about yourself."

Tess started as the shrewd eyes turned to her.

"You'd better write Uncle Luke an autobiography!" Olivia murmured with amusement. "It'll be easier than having to answer a barrage of questions! I *know!* I had to go through it."

"I guess I'm entitled to know something about my relatives—"

"Only you seem to have left it a little late in the day to find out about them!" Ginevra observed.

"All right! All right!" he said testily. "You've had your say over that many times! Well, Tess, what about yourself?"

She said on laughter—

"I'm Johnnie's wife and I've just come out from England."

"Where were you born?"

"In London. My father was a Civil Servant—and a very hard-working one; my mother was musical and dreamed that I might one day be a concert pianist. Only I could never read more than one hand of music at a time, and I liked to play by ear, which is fatal they tell me."

"So what did you do with your life before you married? I hope you worked! I don't like the idea of young people idling around."

Olivia murmured, "Theme No. 1. 'Work my sweeties, work!' "

"What was that?" Luke cupped a hand to his right ear.

"I said we must all work, Uncle Luke," Olivia said suavely and gave him a beautiful smile.

"That's the idea!"

"I was one of the very much under-secretaries for a Cabinet Minister—"

"Were you, now!" He looked at her with interest.

Johnnie, entering the room had heard what Tess said.

"But don't ask her what her politics are, Uncle Luke, because I suspect, like the Vicar of Bray, she would choose them to suit the occasion! Wouldn't you, sweet?"

Tess laughed.

"I wouldn't stand much chance in a political debate, if that's anything to go on! I typed what I was told to type and never felt like giving my life-blood to either side."

"You see," Johnnie said evenly, "I didn't marry a career woman! She'll never be seen arguing her head off on television!"

"Just as well!"

Olivia wandered out of the room and a moment or two later, as old Luke was asking Tess about her stay with Sally in Connecticut, Johnnie broke in saying that he would fetch her last letter in which she told him when she would be arriving in Toronto.

Tess didn't know why, at that moment, she glanced at Ginevra and saw the old eyes follow Johnnie; saw the twist of amusement on the thin dry lips.

He had pulled the living-room door to as he went out, but it remained a little open and through it Tess saw Olivia cross the hall and knew she must be speaking to Johnnie. Well, why not? She told herself that they were cousins and friends; that she had got to accept this family, to live with them, to learn to like them . . . if they would let her. Memory came at that moment of Olivia's cool eyes looking a little down at her from her greater height.

Johnnie came back minutes later, alone. He had Tess' letter in his hands.

"Look," he said, holding it out to her and pointing to a paragraph.

" 'I shall be catching the day train to Toronto on the eighteenth,' " she read.

She stared at her own small, clear handwriting. The figure eighteen was unmistakable, and yet she knew she had never written it. With a queer, cold shiver, she was quite certain that Johnnie had altered it—and she had no way of knowing why. Why hadn't he wanted to meet her? Why hadn't he just written and put her off for two days? Because something had decided him not to meet her at the very last minute, too late to stop her coming. But what?

She felt his eyes watching her and looked up. There was laughter on his face. But there was wariness behind it.

"Darling, you must have been having such a wonderful time with this girl friend, Sally, that you just mixed your dates!"

"But I didn't," she began. I *know*—" and then she stopped because with the evidence in front of her, there was no argument. She let it go. One day, perhaps, she would ask him why he did it. Or perhaps she never would. . . .

III

SOON AFTERWARDS they all went to bed. Old Luke smacked a kiss on Tess' cheek, said, "Nice to have you here, girl."

Ginevra said, "If you want more blankets, there are a couple in the chest in your room."

Olivia did not address her, not even to say good night. She just commented to nobody in particular, "That clock on the mantelpiece is five minutes slow," and walked out.

"Oh, by the way," Tess said, "there's a huge icicle over the porch steps. It scared me—I suppose it couldn't fall—"

"It could." Luke turned to Ginevra. "Have it seen to tomorrow. We don't want a fatal accident on our hands."

The bedroom Tess was to share with Johnnie was a large and beautiful room, furnished in old French provincial style with shiny green and white chintz curtains and bedcover.

Johnnie misinterpreted Tess' gaze.

"Simple, isn't it?" he commented, "unpretentious! But that's Uncle Luke, you'll find. 'Take care of the pennies.' That's his motto." He went to the window. "We look over the drive," he, said. "I've got a sort of study next to this, and there's our own bathroom on the other side, so it's like a suite."

"A study?" Tess asked.

"I'm a working man. I told you in my letter. I'm not to be kept in idleness. It was a matter of what could Uncle Luke find for me to do? He has so many irons in the business fire that it wasn't hard to find something. Since I know a bit about estate work, he's given me a job selling plots up at Lake Chillawoka. He's bought up a huge acreage of land there and plans to turn it into another Muskowka— that's a lake where people pour up for weekends at their summer cottages. My job is to try and charm them into buying. But Uncle Luke doesn't want me working in his office downtown, not yet anyway, so he has fixed up the room next door with a desk and a filing cabinet and that's my study."

"Do you like the work?"

He grinned across the room at her, watching her take off her pearl necklace.

43

"Do I ever like work, sweet? But that's the only way I can stay here. It's the same with Olivia. She's really his wife's niece and she lived in San Francisco. When Uncle wrote and suggested she came up here to live with him and Aunt Ginevra, she found she wasn't to expect to be kept in luxurious idleness. She's very clever, you know, and works on a big newspaper. Sometimes she writes gossip paragraphs for them."

"Did she work in San Francisco before she came here?"

"She did journalistic work there, too."

"And she gave up her home and everything to come here—?"

Johnnie heard the puzzlement in Tess' voice, and laughed.

"You bet she did! Wouldn't you if you were a lone girl earning a tough living and there was a glittering prize luring you like the golden towers in some fairy tale? Olivia has her feet planted firmly on the good earth! She didn't like me at all when I first arrived—she was obviously hoping Uncle Luke would never find his nephew—a whole cake is so much more succulent than half! But I won her around." He grinned at Tess. "You married a man who knows how to handle women, sweet! Uncle Luke is no fool—he'd have smelled out the reason for enmity between us and would probably have sent us both packing!"

"And so you—you and Olivia—are now—good friends!"

"Sure we are—we decided that the gate to the golden city was wide enough for us both! She won't starve, Tess, on half a million dollars; though a cool million would have been sweeter in my fingers!"

Tess slid out of her skirt, pulled her sweater over her head. Shaking her hair, she said:

"There's Aunt Ginevra—"

"Oh, she's got plenty of money of her own from some widower who once wanted to marry her and then died and left her everything. She's alone in the world, so when Aunt Stacey died, Aunt Ginevra came to keep house here. She amuses herself making papier-mâché masks."

"So it's her studio I saw at the back!"

"When did you see it? Oh—of course, when you arrived and found no one to meet you. Poor Tess, what a poor welcome! That'll larn you, sweet, to be careful about dates."

"I was!" She swung around and faced him. "I can almost remember writing the '16th.' "

"But you didn't, did you, or I'd have been at the station and you'd never have had that horrible scare! I suppose it *did* happen? But you didn't imagine it, did you? Uncle Luke will probably go to the police tomorrow and have the street more closely guarded at night." His arm went around her drawing her close. "Still, everything's all right now, isn't it?"

"Of course—" She felt his lips touch hers, his arm tighten and the hard, excited beat of his heart.

Everything's all right! But was it?

Much later, lying in the great bed with Johnnie sleeping by her side, spent with a loving that had found but a small, weary echo in her, Tess felt again the feather of premonition brush her heart.

Why had Johnnie changed the date on her letter? Most certainly not because of a curling match for he could easily have slipped away to meet her, or changed the date openly, telling her the reason. Then why? In that silent night, she could find no answer.

Tess must have eventually slept deeply because when she awoke, she found that Johnnie was not by her side. The curtains were still drawn but she could see that his clothes were gone.

She swung out of bed, slipped her feet into scarlet bunny slippers, slid into a white dressing-gown she had bought in New York and went to the window. In the biting cold outside, the trees seemed to shiver, clouds hung low and new-fallen snow made a frame for the window.

Now she could see the lay-out of Uncle Luke's house. In summer, trees would hide the sight of the other houses, but in winter they showed, large and sumptuous through the bare branches.

Tess held her hands over the hot pipes below the window and watched two small, ear-muffed children in the garden opposite, dragging a yellow sled across the drive.

She was still there when Johnnie walked in. She moved to the dressing table, glancing over her mirrored shoulder, watching his reflection approach her and then felt his face against her hair, his arms crossed over her breast, drawing her back against him.

"When I left, you seemed to be sleeping so peacefully that I didn't have the heart to wake you." He kissed her temple. "Feel refreshed?"

"Yes, thank you."

He drew back, surveying her, his hands tucked into the pockets of his outdoor coat.

"I'd almost forgotten how little you are! My pocket-sized wife!" He measured their heights in the mirror. Then he turned, glanced at his watch and said: "I'm afraid you'll have to breakfast alone. I've got to take some people out to Chillawoka this morning. It's not a good journey in winter, but there you are! People are rushing to buy the best sites—lake view and all that!" he laughed. "You'll find breakfast waiting for you probably in the sun-room. It's all glass, I know, but it's centrally-heated so you won't freeze. There's a maid you'll find somewhere around. She goes by the rich name of Madrigal, and she'll go and tell cook you're ready for breakfast. I must fly now. See you later."

When Tess was dressed, she went down into the hall. Ginevra was standing by a beautiful embroidered screen, and her needle was moving in and out of one corner of the pattern, the gold thread shining as she pulled it taut.

"Ah, Tess, here you are! I hope you had a good night after your miserable welcome;" when she smiled, her face screwed up into a hundred tiny wrinkles, like a walnut shell.

She stuck her needle into the screen, hung her thimble on it and walked to the green baize door, pushing it open and calling.

"Madrigal."

"Yes, ma'am." A gangling young girl with large saucer eyes stood with her long arms at her side, waiting.

"Will you ask cook to get Mrs. Bellairs'

48

breakfast ready? What will you have, Tess?"

She chose a boiled egg and coffee and when Madrigal had scuttled away, Tess stood watching Ginevra return to the screen.

"It's one of the many things Luke found in his second wanderings," she explained. "It comes from China and it is very old. I try to keep it mended as best I can." Her thin, ugly hands moved with beautiful precision over the embroidery. "By the way, after breakfast I'll show you the house. And my studio."

"You make masks, don't you? I saw one last night. The moon suddenly came out and shone right on it."

Ginevra paused and thought, her little light eyes on Tess. "That must be the one I'm working on. It's a mask of one of the musicians in our orchestra out here. An interesting face!" She turned back to the screen. "I see things in faces, you know, things most people don't. I've done all the family except Johnnie and you."

Tess said laughing, "And I'll see awful characteristics in my face that I never dreamed I had!"

"You won't. People are invariably blind to themselves. Other people will see what you don't and what *I* do."

Later that morning, in Ginevra's studio, Tess understood. Standing before the mask of

Luke Bellairs in the crowded studio, she looked at the brilliant likeness and saw things she hadn't noticed in the face of the man himself. There were the blustering handsome features, the smiling bonhomie. But there was also the shrewdness and the hardness that had made his fortune. Animation and vitality had screened in the actual man, the things that were here in the reposed likeness.

"My brother, Tess, is as ruthless as any tycoon over a business deal, but when Sunday comes he'll be bellowing hymns and approving sermons that threaten fire and brimstone to evil doers!" She spoke with a low chuckle as though it amused her. "He's rigid over things like morality and divorce. But he'll strike the hardest bargain in the whole of Toronto."

And it was all there, Tess thought, molded by those long, ugly old fingers.

At last, along a line of unknown faces she saw the mask of Olivia. The brushed-up wings of hair, the fine eyes, the straight nose—everything was there—and more. . . . In profile Olivia's likeness had a ruthlessness, an arrogance; seen full-face it had pride and passion. It wasn't an evil face and yet, in some strange way, it boded evil. Tess shivered.

"I shall do a mask of you soon," old Ginevra was saying.

Mask? Oh, that was the wrong word! The living face was the mask—the modeled likeness the truth . . . !

That day Tess explored Toronto. She walked the streets with their banks of swept-up snow and whenever she felt tired or cold, dived into a drug-store for hot, fortifying coffee.

That night they collected in the living-room, waiting for Angus to arrive. Luke finished his drink and fidgeted, looking at the clock.

"I've got time to make a couple of calls before Dalzell arrives."

Ginevra raised her hooded lids and darted a look at him. "Can't you sit still?"

"No, time's money!" he snapped, and heaved himself out of his chair.

"What hospital is this man Angus Dalzell attached to in Vancouver?" Ginevra moved her gaze to Tess.

"I don't know. He didn't say."

"We'll find out tonight," Luke said. "Great guns, you women! Wanting everyone vetted! I'm going to have a darned good evening of reminiscences—precious few I get here, anyway!—and I don't give a hang if Dalzell practices in the Chinese quarter of Vancouver or among the Indians—he's been East and he's a man who uses his eyes and his brain!

51

Oh, by the way, I reported to the police this morning that Tess thought she heard an intruder here last night. They wanted to come around, but I wouldn't let them. For one thing, nothing has been disturbed, for another there won't be fingerprints. Besides, it's unlikely that we'll all be out of the house at the same time again. They didn't like it much. Guess they enjoy tramping over other folks' places! Anyway, they said they'd have extra watch put on the street." He went to the door, paused and said to Ginevra: "In case I forget to tell you in the morning, I've got Cosmo Rankin coming for dinner tomorrow night."

"Again?"

He quirked a bushy white eyebrow at her.

"I may be in rip-roaring health, but it's time I had my lawyer around to discuss my will."

The door closed.

Olivia took a cigarette from a cherry-wood box and slammed it back on the table.

"I'd like ten dollars for every time he has made that remark to us!"

"Well," Ginevra said calmly, "since his last will left everything to his wife and ghosts don't need money, he'll have to make a new one. You don't dare die intestate when you're worth nearly a million dollars!"

"I don't believe he's going to discuss his

52

will with Rankin! He just enjoys saying that to us, watching the way we sit up, reading our thoughts. 'What's the old man going to leave *me?*' He likes dangling the carrot before the donkey!"

She got up and went to the window, the emerald green skirt of her dress swinging as she walked.

"It's snowing again. You know, Tess, Toronto isn't the best place in the winter. I've got some friends in Montreal who have a sort of guest house for young people—they ski and skate in parties; why not go there for a few weekends? You shouldn't let yourself be stuck here—"

"She might prefer to stay with her husband," Ginevra snapped. "Later they can probably get away together for a week—"

"I was only making a suggestion," she said over her shoulder. "There doesn't seem to be much for her here."

"She's only just arrived! Give her time—"

Olivia turned. She was smiling but not even that lift of her lips could soften her face. She had a beautiful, cold, goddess look as she said:

"I only hope you won't regret coming out here!"

Tess met her gaze calmly. "Why should I? As Aunt Ginevra says, I've got Johnnie."

But a question leapt in her mind even as she

spoke. *Had* she got Johnnie? Would she ever really have him?

There was the sound of a car stopping. Olivia swung back to the window, pulling aside the heavy brocade curtains.

"There he is!"

Tess watched her. She couldn't see Olivia's face, but every line of her body seemed to have sprung alive.

Dinner that night was particularly successful. Luke had found someone who could talk to him knowledgeably about the places he had known. Golden names flowed across the table—Kashmir and Bali, Isfahan and Peking. . . . They swopped experiences over the excellent dinner Mary-Anne Caswall had cooked and afterwards Luke took Angus off to his study to show him his books.

The rest of them watched television. Halfway through the evening Luke poked his head around the living-room door. "Tess—come in here."

She saw Angus in the study standing by a glass case on the wall.

He turned and smiled at her and made a movement, almost as though he would reach out and take her hand.

"I thought you'd like to see something really valuable," Luke said. "That!" and pointed to the tall vase in the locked glass case. "I bought it in Canton and it cost me a small fortune. It's K'ang Hsi and a rare piece at that." He stood rocking to and fro, gazing at it with pride. "Fine, isn't it?"

He unlocked the case and took it out handling it lovingly.

"Look at that work, feel the glaze—like satin, isn't it?"

It was beautiful, a delicate, intricate design of peonies and little bright birds with a background of shining black glaze.

Luke handed it to Angus.

"Know anything about old Chinese porcelain?"

"I knew a man in Peking who had a collection, but I'm no connoisseur."

"But you can tell, can't you, that that's a rare piece? I had it valued by an expert in New York, and the curator of a museum there offered me fifteen thousand dollars for it. But I wouldn't sell. No, sir!"

Luke waited for Angus' admiration like a small boy with a treasured possession.

"You've been to China, Dalzell! Have *you* ever seen a finer piece? Know how they got that glaze? They painted their design of flowers and birds, then filled in the background with black under a coat of transparent green, that's what gives the vase that luminous look."

Angus handed the vase back to the old man. "The Chinese were the best craftsmen in the world in those days." But he spoke abstractedly, as though his mind were on something else, and his eyes were narrowed and hard.

Luke put the vase back into its glass case, locked it and pocketed the keys.

"There you are, Tess," he said to her. "I thought you'd like to see it. I don't often take it out—scared of dropping the durned thing!" he chuckled. "Now Dalzell, about that Manchurian trip of yours—I've got a book somewhere, darned if I know where—" He bent down, running a great finger along one of the crowded lower bookshelves.

Tess sensed that this was dismissal for her. As she opened the study door, she turned to say kindly: "Thank you for showing me that lovely vase," and, as she did so, she caught sight of Angus, standing before it. Once more his expression puzzled her. It was as though he was not just admiring an exquisite piece of K'ang Hsi; it was a cautious, speculative look which she could neither understand nor interpret.

Luke had forgotten her. He was complaining that his books were in a hopeless muddle.

"Over a thousand of them, and I can't put

my hand on anything I want!"

Tess closed the door. She had been called in to see a valuable piece of porcelain, that was all! And yet something troubled her. Why should it matter to her what Angus had been thinking as he stood so silently before that ancient treasure? A whim had induced Uncle Luke to ask him to dinner but after tonight she would never see Doctor Angus Dalzell again.

IV

THE FOLLOWING NIGHT, Luke Bellairs' lawyer, Cosmo Rankin, came to dinner. He was a dried-up little man with a narrow face and pointed ears like a gnome.

After the meal, he went with Luke into the study. Johnnie said he was going to do some work; Olivia was going out to see friends and Ginevra and Tess were left alone in the living-room.

Ginevra switched on the television and played about with it until she found the station she wanted.

"A play," she said, rubbing her long, thin hands, "about Virginia. I lived there for years, you know. By the way, if you'd rather read, Tess, there's the little sitting-room across the hall."

"Thank you. I think I will. I've found a Frances Parkinson Keyes I've never read—"

She went out of the room gratefully; the

play hadn't promised to be particularly interesting to her, and closing the door softly went with her light footsteps across the hall.

She heard the murmur of voices and glancing across the wide hall, saw two people standing close together just inside the little darkened sitting-room. Olivia and Johnnie.

Tess halted.

They were standing close together and as she watched, Johnnie's hand lifted and touched Olivia's hair. It was a light, affectionate gesture; nothing more. But the hand lingered there. Olivia said something, looking up at him and then she put up her own hand and took his.

Johnnie's face bent to hers. And in that moment Tess deliberately dropped the book she had been carrying. It landed with a loud thud on the maple-wood floor. She bent to pick it up and when she looked again, there was no one visible in the little sitting-room.

Shaken, she took a few steps towards it and as she did so she heard a door close. A door where? And then she remembered that when Ginevra had shown her over the house, she had seen two doors leading from the little sitting-room, one into the hall, the other into the passage to the back of the house.

But her quiet read was spoiled. She told

herself that she should have gone boldly, noisily towards them, saying, "Hallo, you two?" not seeing anything significant in their manner. A man talking to his cousin; a light hand placed affectionately on her hair. That was all. Why should she imagine that Johnnie had bent towards Olivia to kiss her? He could have just been saying something quite innocent. What was the matter with her that she was reading more into that small scene than there probably was? Why should she stand there aware of the snake of suspicion creeping around her mind?

She went back into the living-room. Ginevra looked up.

"Changed your mind, Tess? Come and sit down, it's quite a good play."

Changed her mind—or had it changed for her? For no book in the world could hold her attention now. . . .

Her thoughts went on, while her eyes gazed at the bright screen. Johnnie had been out here two months and established himself. These people had shared experiences, cemented friendships. They were his relatives. . . . She must stand guard against jealousy of this beautiful girl who was Johnnie's cousin—cousin far, far removed, she added to herself. . . .

It seemed a very long time after that she

heard Olivia's car start up in the drive.

Ginevra sat remote in her corner of the settee watching, but Tess found the effort to concentrate on a poor play impossible. Upstairs in her room she had a dress she had bought at Saks in New York and which she had not had time to have shortened before she left. Measuring, sticking in pins, sewing—at least it would be activity it would need her whole attention. . . .

Luke always insisted that the television should not blare through the house. If anything was to make a noise, it was his monopoly! So, when Tess was halfway up the lovely, curved staircase she could not hear the voices from the television screen. But in the passage leading to the bedroom there were sounds of two people talking. She heard Luke's roar of laughter, the drone of another voice, then laughter again. And the sounds were coming from Johnnie's study.

Tess paused. Uncle Luke's laughter was infectious. With a gay question ready to be asked: "Can I share the joke?" Tess opened the door of the study.

Johnnie was alone.

He must have sprung up as the handle of the door turned and his outflung hand had sent some papers skimming over the back of the desk. He had reached across to retrieve them as Tess walked in.

"Oh Johnnie—"

He swung around and his face was suddenly a stranger's.

"What the devil do you mean, bursting in here like that?"

"I'm sorry, I thought I heard Uncle Luke's voice. I thought you were having some joke and I—well—I just looked in—" her voice trailed to silence.

"To find out what's going on, I suppose! That's the trouble with women, they must always be in the know!" His eyes blazed at her. "Well, you made a mistake, didn't you? Uncle Luke isn't here. As a matter of fact, I'm working quietly at my desk, my sweet Tess. See—" He flicked some papers; his upper lip parted in a faint sneer.

Tess stared at him.

"Then I must have heard your uncle's voice from the corridor."

"You must! Now for heaven's sake get out and leave me to work."

"Of—course."

But her eyes flashed to the desk and in that moment she saw that the cap was on his pen and there was no pencil in sight. He could have been just reading. Or thinking. . . . It didn't matter any more.

She turned to the door, feeling Johnnie's eyes riveted on her back.

"And in future, this room is mine, do you hear? You come in only when you're invited."

With her hand on the handle of the door, she turned to him. The eyes that looked at her still blazed, his body was rigid with a fury that was out of all proportion to what she had done. Without a word she went through the door and closed it after her.

She stood for a moment in the passage. She must, of course, have heard Uncle Luke's voice from out here. But how could it carry from behind the closed door of his study on the floor below and at the back of the house? There were no voices now. Nobody laughed; nobody spoke. . . .

It no longer seemed to matter. What *did* matter was that she had seen a new Johnnie—and one that frightened her. The gay, charming familiarity was gone and it was as though she was married to a man she suddenly realized she had never really known.

Here in Toronto, she was living among strangers—*all* strangers and there was no one anywhere who could be called her friend. No one! Certainly not in this house with the echoes of voices that came from nowhere and footsteps that padded along dark passages. . . .

Even Angus was just someone she had met on a train; a friend of a friend of a friend far removed from her. What did she know of him save that he had been kind? But Johnnie had been kind once. She knew she must not even trust Angus . . . not yet. And, anyway, she would probably never see him again.

Suddenly Johnnie's door opened.

"I had a feeling you were out here snooping!"

"You're quite wrong. I wasn't even thinking of you!"

"But still listening?"

"No. But still puzzled!" she said with spirit, and forced herself to look at him.

The anger had gone out of his face. Anxiety, pity had taken its place.

"Oh, Tess, watch yourself! Unbridled imagination and suspicion can make people ill. It could be dangerous if you let it get a hold on you. People's minds—"

"My mind is quite all right, thanks!"

"Of course it is!" It was as though he spoke a soothing, pandering lie to a child. "But I can't quite forget that you had a breakdown just before we met. You don't want that to return, do you? You're my wife, Tess dear, I couldn't bear that you get ill again!"

"You seem to have my 'getting ill' on your mind, Johnnie! Don't worry, I feel perfectly well, both physically and mentally."

His eyes narrowed, watching her.

"But you did hear voices, didn't you?"

"I heard them," she almost shouted, "because they were there to *be* heard! For heaven's sake, it's ludicrous for you to think that I came along this corridor and heard imaginary laughter, voices. . . . What *I* heard was definite, Johnnie. Uncle Luke's voice—you can't mistake that! He's no ghost and I have perfectly good hearing—"

"Hush!"

She realized that her voice had risen in agitation and fury. Johnnie laid a restraining hand on her arm and she sprang away as though it had been the touch of a boa constrictor.

"Don't shout," he urged. "You mustn't get excited like this! It's all part of—" He seemed to see some flash in her eyes that silenced him.

"Go on—" she said quietly. "All part of what? What is it you want to believe of me?"

"I want to believe that you're calm and happy, that you're the same girl that I married back in England. I want to believe that this excitability and suspicion is just a phase that will pass. Oh Tess, I want us to be happy!" He spoke with such overwhelming sincerity that she stared at him, almost believing him. He seized his advantage. "Tess dear, try not to get so excited and worked up. It's bad for someone of your temperament."

"You talk as though I were on the razor's edge of insanity!"

"Of course I don't! But isn't it natural that a man should want to take care of his wife, protect her from herself?"

She felt weariness mingle with her anger. The urgency, the fluid speech, the seeming sincerity acted like hypnotism upon her. She saw danger staring at her in his troubled eyes, his soft deadly words and turning, she dashed into her bedroom and slammed the door.

For a shaken moment she leaned against it. *What is happening to Johnnie—to me?*

She pressed her hands to her eyes, but she couldn't shut out Johnnie's face with the feigned pity in it; she couldn't erase the softly insinuating voice. *Wanting to think her unbalanced?* Oh no! If her husband was her enemy, where could she go for trust?

Desperate desire for a friend racked her. Who was there? Uncle Luke? But he was absorbed in his own world and he would have neither patience nor understanding. Aunt Ginevra? But Tess couldn't entirely shut out that first impression of her. Olivia? She was out of the question. Then Angus? Back to Angus. . . .

She stood there aware of the absolute silence of the house. She wondered vaguely what Johnnie was doing in the room behind that closed communicating door. Working? Listening for her? She stared fascinatedly at the door, aware that it was unlocked and that by leaning against the door into the hall she was not barring him from the room.

Where was the Johnnie she had once known, the man she had loved so swiftly, to whom she had been so grateful because he had lifted her finally out of the heavy cloud of shock that had pressed on her after the accident? And why had she told him about that? Why didn't one keep quiet, hold one's counsel instead of wanting to blurt out everything about oneself to the man one loved, as though to say: "Here I am, all of me! The best and the worst. Take me as I am—" Wanting to be honest, not to cheat, not to be taken for a romantic ideal of what one really was! Had Johnnie been as honest with her? She had believed so. Now she was certain that he had come to her charming and gay in those days, but himself a stranger. . . .

V

WHEN JOHNNIE came to bed that night, Tess pretended to be asleep. She had come up early herself saying vaguely that after her week of gay, American nights, she had a lot of sleep to catch up on. She left Johnnie looking at television with the rest of the family and now, as a clock somewhere in the house struck eleven, she heard him close the door and cross the room, standing over her and calling her softly.

"Tess. I want to talk to you."

But her eyelids remained steady over her closed eyes.

"*Tess!*" She felt his hand on her shoulder and went rigid. "I know perfectly well you can't be asleep yet."

She stirred, turned over on her other side, murmuring with exaggerated weariness. "I'm tired! Let me be!"

"But you aren't asleep! Try to gather your

wits and listen. I'm sorry I was angry with you tonight. It was just that I was scared because you seemed so strange; you looked frightened and there was no reason for it. All I said was that I wanted my study to myself. Men do, you know. They like a glory-hole where they can please themselves and not have a woman tidying up after them!"

His tone held almost sweet reasonableness, as though she had only imagined that he had shaken with anger, and had hurled insults and hints at her as though he doubted her sanity! Her eyes remained closed.

"You *are* listening, aren't you, Tess?"

She thought a little hysterically that it was like saying "Die for the Queen!" to a performing dog. He just didn't move, knowing his prize to be a lump of sugar. *Her* prize for lying still would be to be left in peace.

Then, to her relief, she heard Johnnie move away and start to take things out of his pockets. Keys and money clanged on the glass top of the dressing-table; he took his shoes off, tossing them down noisily and she knew—though she dare not look—that he kept glancing at her, hoping for some signal that she was awake.

Dread of having to listen to any more of his curiously gentle and frightening monologue made her lie rigid, aware of her own thudding heart making a drumbeat background to Johnnie's noisy preparations for bed.

Shock at his behavior earlier in the evening had made her cold. The warmth of the room and the bedclothes could do nothing to lessen the iciness of her hands, the slight shivering that swept through her body nor the chilly panic in her heart.

At last he came and lay by her side.

This is Johnnie, this is the man I loved and trusted and wanted to spend the rest of my life with! And now, quite suddenly something was dreadfully wrong.

Their relationship couldn't remain in this half-state; something had to break—or someone. . . .

Presently she heard him breathing deeply and knew that he was asleep. She could open her eyes with safety now. She did so, staring up at the yellow splash of lamplight that shone through a gap in the top of the curtain onto the dark ceiling.

Why should Johnnie remind her, after all this time, of the illness she had had after that fatal accident? When she had told him, he had brushed the whole business aside, saying:

"Shock does odd things to people, sweet! And it was a terrible experience for you. But it's all over now, forget it!"

She had; but it seemed that Johnnie had not! It had been perhaps foolish to have told him; but when you loved someone you wanted to pour out your whole life to them. Like the fairy-tale, you had three gifts to offer—your love, your trust and your life—the past as well as the future.

What had she done tonight to make Johnnie alarmed for her? She had walked into a room with laughter on her lips, wanting to share some joke. That was all! If anyone had behaved strangely it had been Johnnie, and it was she who should be puzzled and afraid. *Should* be? That was the wrong tense—she *was;* her whole being was alert and alive with fear. . . .

At breakfast the next morning everything looked so normal. A family sitting around a table, talking, eating, reading their letters. Yellow and gold china on a snowy cloth; the glint of winter sun on the cut-glass butter dish; the splash of scarlet poinsettias on a table by the window and, outside, the snow like a bridal gown over the hushed garden. There was nothing to be afraid of; nothing sinister here. . . .

Vaguely she listened to the talk around the table. Uncle Luke was saying that when spring came, he must take Johnnie up to Yellowknife with him to see the mines there; Olivia was looking through a store's catalogue, gloating a little over the photograph of a white fox stole. Johnnie was being gay, teasing his aunt who was asking him when he would sit for a mask.

"I charge highly for sittings, Aunt Ginevra!" he laughed. "Ten dollars a time. But then think how outstanding my face will be among all the other masks in your studio!"

Newspapers rustled, conversation flowed in brief snatches; Madrigal brought in fresh toast, a second egg for Uncle Luke. Sinister? This house? These people? Tess could almost laugh at herself as she watched them in this morning brightness.

Presently Luke gulped down the last of his coffee, lit one of his obnoxiously strong cigarettes and rose from the table. He dived for the door, his great shoulders seeming to precede him.

Then he paused.

"Oh, Ginevra, that young man Dalzell has offered to rearrange and catalogue my books. I've decided that the small cloakroom off my study can be turned into an annex for that overflow I've got in crates down in the cellar. I'll get a carpenter in to make shelves. Meanwhile get Mary-Anne or Madrigal to show Dalzell where the books are stored. I don't know when he'll come."

"Goodness me!" Ginevra protested. "Why on earth does a complete stranger want to take on a job like that? Or are you paying him well?"

"It's costing me nothing," the old man said with satisfaction. "It's purely voluntary and he suggested it. He'll enjoy the job. I've told him he can take all the time he likes over it and that means be can browse till his eyes pop out!"

"But hasn't he got a job of work to do?"

"He's still on sick leave, and like me, he hates to be idle!"

Three pairs of eyes looked at Luke in one consolidated gaze. It said as clearly as words: "Opening your doors to a stranger? You must be in your dotage!"

The great man grinned at them, let out a coil of strong smoke, and said:

"Got work to do! So long, folks!"

The door slammed behind him.

Three pairs of eyes moved to Tess.

"Well, I'm damned!" Johnnie broke the silence. "You've started something, Tess! Who is this Dalzell? Little Lord Bountiful? Some overgrown Boy Scout doing his great good deed? Or a confidence man?"

"I think," Olivia drawled, "that Dr. Dalzell's

dark blue eyes have hypnotized Uncle Luke. But people don't go around doing good deeds, not to rich men—unless they have an ulterior motive."

"Perhaps"—Tess found herself defending Angus—"it's just as simple as Uncle Luke says. Perhaps he just loves to browse through books about the East—and here's a glorious chance."

She caught the look that flashed between Olivia and Johnnie but couldn't define it—it was meaningful and secret and it lingered just a little too long. . . .

Tess was helping to clear the table when Johnnie emerged from the enormous cupboard where the men's outdoor coats and the family's overshoes were kept.

"Oh Tess—"

She waited.

"I don't know if you were really asleep last night when I came to bed but if you were, I want to say how sorry I am about what happened. I shouldn't have been so angry with you—"

"I heard everything you said then, Johnnie. There's no need to go over it again."

Someone was opening the front door. It closed and the inner door opened. Olivia rushed in the hall. She wore a lynx coat and a green headscarf and she looked impatient and angry.

"Something's gone wrong with the ignition of my car," she said to Johnnie. "I'll have to ring the garage when I get to the office—I can't stop now or I'll be late. Could you drive me downtown?"

"Of course. Are you ready?"

"Yes."

"So am I. Come on, let's go."

Tess was at the green baize door. She thought Johnnie called "Good-bye," but she made no answer and the door swung softly behind her as she went into the noise and clatter of the kitchen.

Mary-Anne Caswall liked no one in her kitchen but Madrigal, whom she could order about, like a child. Tess set down the things she had brought from the dining-room and returned to the hall. It was very quiet, this side of the green door. The only sound she could hear was Luke telephoning in his study. She waited, plucking at drooping blooms in the great vase of flowers on the hall-table and when she no longer heard his voice on the telephone, she knocked on the study door.

Luke was heaving himself into his outdoor coat.

"I'd like to know if you can find any work

75

for me to do——"

"Girl," he interrupted, "You must be a thought-reader! I was going to find you something. As you know, I don't like to see young people hanging around. Time's meant to use, not waste!"

"I'm a good shorthand-typist——"

"I've got an army of them down at my office. And anyway, it's a bad thing to bring in a relative and make a temporary job for her; causes discontent among the permanent staff. If you like, you can help me here at home. There's a typewriter on that table in the corner. I'll give you some personal work to do. It won't keep you busy all day and every day, but it'll be better than nothing." He looked at his watch. "I'll leave you some work on that desk."

"Thank you." She turned to go.

Luke said, "You like it here?"

"It's a wonderful country."

"You haven't seen it yet; but it is. I mean, do you like living here with us?"

"Yes. Oh yes," she said politely and untruthfully.

"That's fine. I like having you. I'm glad Johnnie's married to a nice steady girl."

Tess made the bed in her room, and heard old Luke leave, with much stamping and bustle and slamming of doors, for his office.

When she went downstairs again, the front door was open. Madrigal stood there, her head outlined in golden light. The snow dazzled Tess' eyes and then, as the door closed, she could see clearly again who had entered.

"Hallo, Tess," said Angus and stood in the hall waiting for her.

Madrigal scuttled away flapping a vivid purple duster.

Angus said:

"You knew about my coming, didn't you?"

"Yes. Uncle Luke told us this morning," she laughed, "but it's barely ten o'clock! You seem keen to get on with the job!"

"You've no idea how I'm looking forward to wallowing through all those books!" He turned as Ginevra, light as a wraith, a cardigan slung across her bent back, came through the green-baize door.

"Ah, Dr. Dalzell. We know all about your coming." She raised her heavy-lidded eyes and her look was ironic and penetrating. "I can only hope you realize what you've taken on!"

"I think I do."

"Well, there's the study. We've had a pair of steps put in there so that you can reach the top shelves. And there are pens, pencils, and a heap of paper for you."

"Thank you. I shall roll my sleeves up and

get down to it."

As he went towards the study Ginevra beckoned Tess, took her into the small sitting-room and pushed the door to.

"Are you going to be in this morning?"

"Yes. Uncle Luke has found some work for me to do."

"Good, because I have to go out and I don't like a strange man being left in the house, most certainly not after what happened the other night."

"Angus and I have mutual friends. Don't worry, Aunt Ginevra."

"Youth these days accepts too much at face value! The world is full of adventurers and men who seize an easy opportunity. Luke's knowledge of people has been sound all his life, but he's getting old and his judgment may be slipping."

"He doesn't give the impression of it!" Tess said lightly.

"Maybe not. But why on earth should a perfect stranger volunteer to catalogue a library?" She rubbed her thin hands together. "Ah well, so long as one of us is always around while he's here. I have shopping to do."

After Ginevra had gone Tess stared at the delicate tracery of the branches against the blue winter sky beyond the porch. She heard the domestic noises of the house; the drone of the Hoover; someone moving about in the room above and the thud of a bed being pulled out. A tradesman came up the drive with bread.

She was trying to make sense of the curious feeling of security that had come to her with the knowledge that Angus was in the house.

But she knew she had got to reassure the family about him, and there was one way to do that. She went back to her room, got out her writing-case and wrote to Sally. She had already sent her "thank you" letter and had told her of meeting Angus on the train. Now she carried on from there, telling Sally how Angus was to become a frequent visitor to the house for some time, and that old Luke had taken a great fancy to him. "But we seem to know so little about him," she went on, "except that he's a doctor and has traveled a lot. The family are queasy about having such a total stranger walking in and out of the house but they never cross Uncle Luke! I wish I could quote from someone who knows Angus and his background, and put the family's mind at rest."

She made a question of it all, so that Sally would feel bound to answer.

Because Angus was using the study, Tess

decided to work in the little sitting-room. She slipped out and posted her letter and then went to collect the typewriter.

She found Angus perched on the step-ladder with books piled on the magnificent desk. But he wasn't working. He was looking up, with narrowed, thoughtful eyes, at the K'ang Hsi vase.

He slid off the ladder as Tess entered. She crossed the room and stood in front of the glass case.

"It is lovely, isn't it?"

Light glowed on the clear colors of the peonies and the birds; the black glaze had the sheen of water. Craftsmen dead for over a thousand years had put all their pride and their love into the fashioning of it. And yet, for Uncle Luke it represented not so much a beautiful and beloved work of art, but fifteen thousand dollars. . . .

Tess asked: "Do you like old things; old china, old glass?"

"Yes—" He was still frowning.

"But you don't seem to like that much!"

He turned and looked at her. "In a way, I don't."

"But why? It's so beautiful."

"Yes, but it isn't what it's supposed to be."

"Angus, what *do* you mean?"

"Perhaps I should keep my mouth shut—perhaps this is where ignorance, like the proverb says, should be bliss!"

"Are you trying to break something to me gently, something about the vase? Is it cracked or chipped?"

He said, "No, Tess, I was arguing inside myself as to whether I should tell you—" He paused, walked to the window and back again, not seeming to see her, absorbed in his decision. Then he said quietly: "You see, that vase is a work of art in its way. But it isn't a K'ang Hsi. It's just a most beautiful copy!"

She stared at him.

"But how *could* it be? Uncle may know nothing about old porcelain but you've seen him—he's not the sort of man to be fobbed off with a fake."

"Perhaps I shouldn't have told you. But I think someone in the family should know, and decide whether to tell your uncle."

"But how can you be sure since you said last night you knew nothing much about these things?"

"I told your uncle I'd seen some K'ang Hsi in Peking. A very old and cultured Chinese I met showed me his collection. He told me at the time that a firm in Paris had made copies—very fine ones, magnificently produced and never with the intention of passing them off as originals. But less scrupulous people who bought them have tried just that!"

"Was there some mark on the originals that you didn't see on this one when you looked at it?"

"No, old Chinese craftsmen never marked their work. But I looked inside that vase, Tess. Genuine K'ang Hsi pieces have a touch of gray in the whiteness. The copies are much clearer and purer in color. This one your uncle has is very white indeed."

She stared at him in dismay. "What do we do now?"

"I can do nothing. I've told you, it's for you to decide."

She said slowly, thinking aloud:

"Suppose Uncle Luke knows it isn't genuine, and is just pretending, having us all on, because he's quite certain no one he shows the vase to will know the real from the copy? On the other hand, if he bought it for a genuine K'ang Hsi, perhaps it would be best not to tell him because his vanity would be so hurt. And what does it matter, anyway, so long as he thinks it's genuine?"

"Either way argues in favor of our saying nothing, doesn't it? Truth that isn't palatable is usually best left unsaid."

"If it were me, I'd always rather know the truth!"

"Would you?" His disconcerting gaze met hers. "Whatever that truth was, *would* you prefer to know it?" Not only his voice, but his expression, struck a chord of alarm inside her. She had a feeling that he had forgotten the vase, that this question was essentially personal and concerned just the two of them.

"Would you want to know the truth at any price, Tess?"

She felt his eyes steady and asking on her face and, without reason, her blood began to race suffusing her throat and cheeks.

She couldn't answer him! Some strong emotion whipped the power of speech from her. "What is this man doing to me? What hidden meaning is in his question?" Or was all this her imagination, heightened by her own emotion and unhappiness? That must be it. She took hold of herself. *For heaven's sake, don't go seeing significance in every word Angus tosses at you! You'll be seeing ghosts soon, and hearing voices! Hearing voices. . . .* But she had.

"You want that typewriter moved into another room? I'll take it for you."

The moment of strong emotion was over. She turned her burning face away.

"Thank you, Angus. It's to go in the little

sitting-room across the hall."

He carried it for her and set it down on a table near the window, and said lightly:

"I hope you enjoy your morning's work!"

"I don't suppose I'll enjoy it as much as you!" She was steady again now; she could talk naturally and even laugh. "Typing 'Dear Mr. Jones' and 'I am, yours etc.' isn't as exciting as reading about the elephants of Katmandu or the native bazaars in Rangoon!"

Pale primrose sunlight from outside lit up his face and she saw the furrow between his brows deepen.

"I wonder," he said slowly. "I wonder, Tess, if I'm doing the right thing. Or if I'm making a mistake I'll regret all my life."

He allowed her no time to question. "What mistake? What will you regret?" Almost before he had finished speaking he was out of the room and the door closed quietly behind him. . . .

VI

TESS DIDN'T SEE Angus again that morning. She heard Madrigal take him in some coffee at about half-past eleven and just before lunch she saw him walking down the drive, hands in his pockets, head bent against the icy wind that blew straight and clean and without mercy from the Arctic Circle.

Tess was restless in this house where only old Luke seemed unaware of tension, and after lunch she went out to explore Casa Loma, that strange dream castle in the center of Toronto with its secret staircases and hidden panels. Then she found a place for tea, suffered the inevitable tea-bag in hot water, and afterwards went for the second time to the Art Gallery.

By the time she returned home she realized she had walked some miles and was tired. She collected the work she had done for Luke and, taking it to his study, found Olivia there sorting a great pile of magazines and papers. She looked up casually, without interest, glanced at the papers in Tess' hand and said:

"Oh hallo! Has Uncle Luke got you earning your keep, too?"

"I asked him for something to do."

A touch of malicious amusement crossed Olivia's beautiful face.

"You catch on quickly, Tess! Clever girl! So you've found that the way to Uncle's heart is through working for him? Well! Well!" her eyes flicked over the small, slender figure with faint insolence. "How deceptive you are, my dear!"

"Am I?" Tess asked lightly. "What do I seem to you, then, Olivia? A mouse?"

"No, but romantic and—er—gently so-phisticated if you get my meaning. You can't be naïve or Johnnie would never have mar-ried you—"

"Thanks for the analysis of my character," Tess cut in dryly. "So far as the job for Uncle Luke is concerned, I wanted something to do for my *own* sake. The housework is all done for us here and I can't just idle the time away."

"*I* could!" Olivia dragged out a magazine from the pile. "I don't know why, but every bit of printed matter in this house seems to find its way into this study! I suppose it's that moron, Madrigal, who imagines that nobody can read but Uncle Luke!"

Tess moved away from the big carved desk and as she turned, the K'ang Hsi vase drew her gaze. Genuine or a copy? Which?

"I know just what you're thinking," Olivia observed. "All that money shut up in a glass case! And Uncle Luke crooning over it like a child!" She glanced at her beautiful dark reflection in a mirror by the door, ran a palm over one black wing of hair and her eyes slid over her shoulder to Tess' reflection. "I heard once how much insurance Uncle pays for that vase!"

Insurance! Tess hadn't thought of that! Uncle Luke, then, believed it genuine if he had insured it heavily. Well, it was nothing to do with her—she would keep her own counsel.

"If Uncle made me a gift of that vase," Olivia went on, "I'd sell it to a museum and buy a whole wardrobe of beautiful clothes—a platinum-mink coat—"

"Oh, but it wouldn't buy you *that!*"

For a moment, silence hung about the room. In horror Tess realized that, taken off her guard, she had given away the secret she and Angus had decided to keep. Words had burst involuntarily from her.

"What do you mean?" Olivia had swung away from the mirror, one hand still arrested in its movement towards the door.

"Nothing. Nothing at all!" If Olivia would only move, she could make a dive for that door and escape. . . .

"Now look, Tess, don't make statements and then try to retract! What did you mean by inferring that that vase wasn't worth much?"

"As I know nothing about old porcelain—"

"What did you mean?" Olivia's eyes were like fire, ready to burn an explanation out of her.

Tess knew she was caught.

"Just suppose," she said helplessly, "that it is just a copy!"

"Someone has put that thought in your mind. Now who?" She leaned up against the wall, eyes thoughtful, watching Tess. "But of course, it can only be your doctor friend, Angus Dalzell. That's it, isn't it?" She waited. "What did he actually say?"

Tess threw a question back. "Do *you* think that vase is genuine?"

"Yes, because I know the firm from whom Uncle Luke bought it—they have too good a reputation to palm anyone off with some mere copy."

"Then there's nothing more to say. I'm sure you're right and it's a genuine piece." She hoped she spoke with conviction, but Olivia was too sharp.

"Angus said it wasn't genuine, didn't he?

How does he think he knows? Come on, Tess, tell! You'd better because I'll find out sooner or later." When she smiled, her crimson-painted lips seemed to stretch tightly over small white teeth. "Well?" She waited.

Tess gave in. She had said so much, she might as well tell everything.

"Genuine K'ang Hsi have a slightly grayish tinge to the white. The copies are much clearer in color. This one is."

Olivia looked up at it speculatively.

"Your friend Angus has quite a point!" she said at last. "I wonder what we'd better do."

"Perhaps Uncle Luke knows it's only a copy and is having a lovely game pretending it is genuine."

"There are all manner of possibilities! I think we'll just leave it, shall we?" It was more like a command than a question. "So, don't go telling anyone else what you've told me."

"Angus could be wrong! I'd like," Tess said with conviction, "to forget all about it!"

"Do then, dear." Olivia flashed a smile at her.

It didn't really matter, Tess told herself, that Olivia knew. In a way she was glad; though she was angry at herself for blurting out something she had meant to keep to herself, like a child unable to hold a secret! What was the matter with her? What force here was stronger than herself?

However, now someone in the family knew about the Chinese vase and the responsibility was out of her hands. Olivià could do what she liked. Tell Uncle Luke, tell Ginevra. She had a strong feeling that if she told anyone, it would be Johnnie. . . .

Two days later, a letter came from Sally Burns and Tess opened it at the breakfast table.

It covered three pages and the last paragraph concerned Angus.

"When we got your letter, Bill rang his friends and asked about Angus. They said they'd met him for the first time in New York, and they knew very little about him except that he's a very nice man. So Bill called a doctor friend of his who lives in Vancouver and he said that the name Angus Dalzell wasn't on the list of medical men in the city. So you know as much about him as we do!"

"What is it, Tess? Bad news?"

Ginevra's question cut through her faint shock. She realized that she must have been staring in dismay at the letter in her hands.

"It's from Sally, the friend I stayed with in Sarraway Fields."

"Well, you look as though you'd seen a ghost, or read about one!" Olivia observed.

Tess folded her letter quietly, thinking,

90

"She doesn't like me; she never will!" But somehow that wasn't important in the light of the fact that there was no Dr. Angus Dalzell in Vancouver. . . .

And then she felt the family's eyes on her and caution made her smile brightly. Whoever Angus was, *whatever* he was, she clung to her faith in him because he was the rock in this drowning sea of strangers.

Johnnie was saying that he'd be home to lunch.

"There's nothing much for me to do today, is there, Uncle Luke?"

"You'd better come down to the office with me this morning and we'll see."

He grinned wryly, gave a little mock salute and said: "Aye! Aye, sir!"

"I'm leaving now, so finish your coffee and get a move on!"

"I'd like to do something about those files in your study, Uncle Luke," Tess said.

"You do that then, girl! And there's some typing I'll leave you. It's just a batch of stuff I must send to my lawyer, but I want to keep copies for myself."

Angus hadn't arrived when Tess went into the study. She took out the first folder, saw that "A's" and "B's" were muddled up, papers were crumpled where Luke had jammed them in with his characteristic impatience and there was one ludicrous "Z" among them.

When Angus arrived, she would leave this job and carry on with the typing, in the meantime she could see hours of work here.

She had reached the "C" folder when she found a letter from the lawyer, Rankin, creased and a little tattered. She stood, smoothing it out, and Johnnie's name sprang at her from the page. It was a report that the firm had traced a John Bellairs to Mexico City, and then lost track of him.

Tess frowned, wondering why Johnnie had never mentioned that he had ever been to Mexico. It seemed there was still so much that she didn't know about him, of his life as well as of himself, the real Johnnie behind the charming exterior! She put the letter in its right folder and heard voices outside in the hall.

Then the study door opened. She swung around, expecting Angus. But Johnnie stood there, bright-eyed, watching her.

"Hallo, my working wife! What are you doing?"

"Tidying Uncle Luke's appalling files," she replied.

"Well, drop it. I haven't anything to do this morning so I thought we'd go downtown and do some shopping. I want to get a couple of new ties. You can finish that job this afternoon."

She pushed the big drawer to and turned to him.

"Johnnie—"

"Uh-huh?"

"I came across a letter from Rankin, Uncle Luke's lawyers. It said they had traced you to Mexico City and then lost track. I didn't know you'd ever been there."

Immediately she knew she had said the wrong thing. The laughter went out of his face.

"Well, why should you know? What's important about it, anyway?"

"Nothing, only, if a man's been to a foreign country he usually talks about it some time or other."

"Tells his wife all; lays his whole life bare for her to peer into! Is that it?"

She heard the faint sneer in his voice and said quickly:

"Now you're going to extremes!"

" 'What did you have for dinner on March the tenth, nineteen sixty-four?' 'How many girls did you date before me?' 'Why did you?' 'How did you?' 'When did you?' Well, shall I write a detailed autobiography for you."

"Johnnie, you're being absurd!" she cried. "I made a simple statement—merely that I didn't know you'd ever been to Mexico City."

"Well, I have. Do you want proof? Shall I tell you about it?"

"No, I don't want to hear."

"But you shall," he said softly and came towards her. "You shall, Tess. I was there five years ago doing a job of work for the Palace of Fine Arts. I stayed with a family in a Spanish-colonial house in Coyoacán. I had some snapshots of myself taken leaning up against a palm tree outside the Cathedral, picnicking at the Floating Gardens, and even one taken at the Casuelas, where I took a pretty Mexican girl, whose name I've forgotten, to dinner. *Now* do you believe me?"

"You didn't have to go to such efforts to prove it!"

"Oh, but it seems I did!"

Suddenly he reached out and gripped her arms. "This is the second time in a few days that you've shown suspicion of me! What's the matter with you? What's at the back of that odd mind of yours?"

She met his furious eyes without flinching.

"The other day, I walked into your study because I thought you and Uncle Luke were having a joke together. Today, I was merely surprised that you hadn't told me you'd been in Mexico City. If you can make something dramatic out of those, then it's your mind that's odd, not mine!" She gave a little cry as his fingers tightened on her arms. "And please let go, you're hurting me!"

"Perhaps that's the only way to bring you to your senses!"

Her calmness seemed to increase his fury. He began to shake her so hard that she cried out.

"I won't put up with an inquisitive, spying wife, do you hear? *Do you hear?*"

"I beg your pardon!" said a quiet voice behind them.

Johnnie dropped his hands and swung around. Angus stood quite still in the doorway.

"I hope I'm not intruding."

"You damned well are!" Johnnie shouted. "What do you want here?"

"To get on with the job I've offered to do." Angus made no move to go away. He stood just inside the door and his eyes never left Johnnie's face.

"I see, then, that it's *we* who are intruding! *I* beg *your* pardon!" Johnnie said with heavy sarcasm. "Come, Tess, we'll go and do that shopping."

"I have work to do," she said quietly, wanting more than anything to get away and rub her bruised and burning arms.

"I told you, you can do that this afternoon."

"I shall do it now. You must shop alone."

She moved towards the door, passing both men without a glance, crossed the hall and went into the little sitting-room, locking the door behind her.

She stood, leaning against the table and heard footsteps cross the hall. The door handle rattled.

"Tess! Tess, what's the matter with you? Open this door!"

She didn't answer.

"Tess—"

"Go away!" she said loudly. "Go away, Johnnie!"

She listened and heard, with relief, his footsteps re-cross the hall. There was silence for a few minutes and then the front door closed. She saw Johnnie walk down the drive, turning once to look at the curtained window behind which she stood.

But Tess couldn't settle to work. She walked the room, smoking one cigarette after another without enjoyment, scarcely even noticing what she was doing.

Johnnie *had* been to Mexico City—he had proved that to her by what he had told her. Then why behave as he had when she asked him about it? Why answer some quite innocent questions with violence?

If only I could get back to England, she thought in despair. But she had no money of her own and she knew there was no one in this house who would help her leave Johnnie.

Perhaps he wanted her to go! The thought deepened, took shape. Perhaps he was trying to frighten her away—wanting to find her unbalanced; wanting to sow the seed of doubt about her instability. . . . That glimpse she had had of Olivia and Johnnie in this very room, in the dark, standing very close. . . . Olivia's hand touching Johnnie's; his head bending to hers before Tess had deliberately disturbed them. Perhaps, during the two months he had lived in this house, Olivia with her beauty and her powerful personality had caught at his imagination and infatuated him. He wouldn't dare let anyone know in case his uncle should find out. Ginevra had called old Luke "narrow and puritan in outlook, declaiming divorce as one of the great sins." If Johnnie wanted to be free of Tess to marry Olivia then he would run the risk of being disinherited. But if he could scare Tess away so that he was the innocent one, the one sinned against, that would be another matter! Was that the explanation? Did they meet downtown, loving secretly, laughing at their cleverness, planning for the future. . . .

Tess found that she was crying; tears pressed out of her eyes with a deep, inner pain. This explanation for all that happened since she had come to the Bellairs house was, on the face of it, a likely one. And yet, as she leaned there against the table, it seemed too obvious a one, almost too naïve. . . .

Something else, something far more sinister might lie behind Johnnie's anger. One day, she was certain, she would know; she would *have* to know—whether she wanted to play ostrich or not—because nothing in life stood still. Events stormed on to their inevitable climax, lifting you or breaking you. . . .

There was a knock on the sitting-room door. Tess unlocked it and then sat in the chair in front of the typewriter and busied herself with papers, calling "Come in."

Madrigal entered with a little tray of coffee and a tiny jug of cream.

"M's Ginevra says, you want some cookies, ma'am?"

"No thank you, Madrigal."

"The gen'leman in the study, he say no, too!" Madrigal said in her sad, sing-song voice. "They'm good cookies, ma'am."

"I'm sure they are, but I had a big breakfast," Tess said kindly.

When the door was closed she turned gratefully to the steaming, fragrant drink. An idea struck her that she might do something to her face and then take her coffee into the study and join Angus. But caution stopped her. She did not know yet whether she could trust Ginevra Bellairs and she was perfectly certain nothing escaped those watchful, hooded eyes.

She sat staring over the porch to the wide, beautiful street with its opulent houses glimpsed now through the bare branches of the trees.

If only there was someone in the whole of Toronto to whom she could go and talk; if only she dare take Angus into her confidence! But you couldn't go to a man you scarcely knew and say: "My husband is acting strangely and, it may sound silly, but I'm afraid of him. There's no one in the family I can talk to about it. I don't trust the beautiful girl who is his cousin, nor Aunt Ginevra, who makes masks of people and looks a bit like one of Macbeth's witches . . . !"

Again, if she could go to Angus, what advice could he possibly give her? Yet she knew that just to talk to him, to be near him, would be to feel his quiet strength flowing through her. She leaned back in her chair and closed her eyes and could feel again the strong magnetism, the pulsing excitement that had swept her only yesterday as she had stood near him in Luke's study.

But Angus was a stranger and one day his work here would be finished and he would never come back again. . . .

How far away was London, how unreal the old love! She thought again, with incredulity, how Johnnie had changed. Or had he? He had been gay in those days, they had laughed together and talked about themselves. But looking back, she felt now that even in those days there had been a shutter that had prevented her from knowing too much of Johnnie. She had been too much in love to see it then, now she realized all too clearly that he had from the very beginning kept something of himself from her. . . .

Love shattered, doomed and bedeviled by doubts. . . . A dark star most certainly shone when she was born. . . .

VII

ON SATURDAY MORNING the whole family was at home.

Olivia rose late and drifted around the house in a pair of russet velvet slacks and an orange blouse. She looked like a beautiful gypsy. From the kitchen came the sound of music, faint and indistinguishable through the baize door. Luke was in his study, occasionally appearing in the hall to roar an order to Ginevra who listened and obeyed in her own sweet time, or to Madrigal, who scuttled like a scared bird to do what she was told.

It was Olivia's task, Tess soon learned, to do the flowers. They would be delivered every Saturday and she would carry them, together with the great white urn, the bronze bowl and the green jars, to the small washroom near the kitchen.

She had a way with flowers and a fine eye

for line and color. Hot-house gladioli were arranged with plumes of pale pampas grass and silvery dried castor-bean leaves; roses bloomed crimson among dark green pine branches and she had also collected a heap of summer and autumn flowers which she had dried up in one of the attics. Blue delphinium and golden rod; beech leaves and blue sage and celosia; fern and rose-tinted strawflowers. She was humming a catchy tune she could hear from Mary-Anne Caswall's kitchen radio as she worked, and Tess, passing on her way to the kitchen, paused and watched her.

"They're lovely!" she said warmly.

"I studied flower arranging in San Francisco," she said in her drawling voice.

"I'd love to go there, it sounds a most exciting city."

"It is." She snapped the stem of a fern and set it in place in the blue jar, low down, splaying over the rim. "I can't wait to get back."

"I thought you were going to stay here for good—"

Tawny-gold eyes glanced with amusement at Tess.

"That's a very elastic expression. 'For good' can mean for just so long as things remain as they are—a year, five years—well, if it's as long as that, I'm young, I can wait!"

Tess knew what she meant. She was staying here in the Toronto house for as long as Uncle Luke lived. She was staying in order to keep her eye on her half of a million dollars! She might hate it here, away from all her friends, away from the beautiful city on the Pacific coast, but she would not make any move that might lose her her inheritance.

Tess had that morning received her small allowance from Johnnie and was going downtown. She had seen a small statuette of a girl with a little cat in her arms in a shop on Bloor Street which she wanted to send to Sally for her birthday.

The hall was empty as she passed Olivia on her way from the kitchen and she let the green door swing to behind her shutting out Olivia's soft singing and the radio accompaniment. She was halfway upstairs when the telephone began to ring.

The study door opened and Ginevra came out and went towards the kitchen door with some household account books in her hand. Luke's voice boomed from his study.

"Anyone out there?" He came to the door. "Ginevra? Tess? Oh there you are! Go up and tell Johnnie there's a call for him—long distance. I'm off out and he'd better take it in my study. Tell him to step on it!"

With flailing arms, he struggled into his coat and strode to the, front door, jamming his hat on his head as he went.

Tess ran up the stairs calling Johnnie.

"It's long distance—"

"Coming." He shot out of his room, passing Tess on the landing, and raced down to the study.

Tess went into the bedroom and put on a thick tweed coat and a small, sky-blue, tight-fitting cap.

Out on the landing again, she heard voices coming from Johnnie's study. The door was open and the room was empty. *And yet there were voices. . . .*

Almost forcibly pushed by curiosity, Tess defied Johnnie's order and went in. She heard Johnnie speaking, and the sound was very slightly distorted, but unmistakable.

"Yes. Yes, that's fine! On Thursday, then, I'll pick you up soon after eleven and run you out to Entobicoke. Fine. . . ! Good-bye." The telephone clicked.

Tess stood motionless. Why could she hear so distinctly all that was said in Uncle Luke's study? Did noises rise through the chimney? This was one of the older houses of Toronto and the fireplace was enormous; but that didn't explain it. Then suddenly she heard

Johnnie's voice again.

"Oh hallo, Olivia?"

"Johnnie dear—" the voice purred. "I've got something to tell you, something that may startle you."

"What?"

"That Chinese vase—did you think it was genuine?"

"Of course."

"Well, it isn't! Angus Dalzell told Tess—"

"What the devil does he know about it?"

"It seems he knows quite a bit! It's got something to do with the color of the glaze inside. Apparently copies were made some time early this century by a firm in Paris, oh quite aboveboard! But they're so beautifully done that they are almost unrecognizable from the real—"

There was a moment's silence. Then Johnnie said:

"But good heavens, if this is true—"

"It means that fifteen thousand dollars has gone into something worth only a few hundred! Or do you think Uncle Luke bought a genuine one and someone has replaced it with a not very valuable copy?"

"How could they?"

"Yes, Johnnie dear, how *could* they? It's tempting fate, though, isn't it, to flaunt a museum piece in front of all and sundry who come here? And Tess is quite certain she heard someone in the house on that night she arrived—someone who shouldn't have been here! I wonder who?"

"She could have made it up, just to seem important! But never mind that now! The question is the vase. What do we do?"

"We can do just nothing, Johnnie."

"You mean let Uncle Luke think he bought an original?"

"But I believe he did! Don't you, *really?*"

"How in the world can I know?"

A little chuckle, low and faintly malicious, crept into the room.

"So shall we keep it as our secret, Johnnie dear?"

"How can we when Dalzell knows, and Tess?"

"But perhaps they don't know quite as much as we do?"

"What in the world are you talking about?"

There was a pause. Then: "Johnnie," Olivia said in a clear, firm voice. "We're going to be rich one day, aren't we?"

"You bet we are!"

"But half isn't as good as the lot, is it—*the whole beautiful lot of lovely money!*"

Her expression must have told him what she meant for Tess heard him exclaim:

"You should burn for a witch, Olivia! A—lovely—witch—"

Tess knew that note of deep urgency in Johnnie's voice. She had heard it so often in the past—it was a sound torn from a state of high emotion.

"Come here, Olivia."

"Johnnie—*darling*—"

There was a pause, a whisper.

Suddenly movement came back to Tess. She walked over to Johnnie's desk which stood slantwise, cutting off the corner between the fireplace and the window. She leant over and there, well hidden, she saw a tape recorder.

Her fascinated eyes followed the line of electric cord which went to the fireplace and disappeared up it. Somewhere in that chimney there was a connection with the chimney and the room downstairs. She had no idea how it was done, but Johnnie, mechanically minded, had found a way to listen in to and record the conversations in the study below. But what was he listening for? And why?

Voices were talking again. Tess had missed a lot. Now she heard Olivia saying:

"We've got to have no secrets from one another. First we've got to talk about—"

"My God!" Johnnie broke in. "I forgot—"

There was a sudden rush of sound as though Johnnie had flung himself across the room below, a protest from Olivia, the opening of the study door.

Tess fled from the room, ran down the passage, and went on shaking legs down the stairs and saw Johnnie at the bottom. She looked straight down at him; direct into his eyes. And she knew that *he* knew where she had been! In his dash to answer the telephone, he had forgotten to turn off the tape-recorder and his door had been left open. Now, as he saw Tess, he knew he had remembered too late. . . .

She tried to pass him in the hall, but his hand shot out and held the newel post, blocking her way.

"Where have you been?"

She couldn't look at him.

"Getting my hat and coat."

"But not just that! *Where have you been?*" He waited, watching her. "Or shall I tell *you?* You're no actress, my dear! You give yourself away. You've been to my study again! And I told you not to, didn't I? Well, why did you go in? And what are you looking like a hunted hare for?" He was speaking quietly, his eyes like points of steel.

"I'm not frightened, Johnnie. But I'm—shocked!"

"Why?"

"I *did* go into your study—and I heard—"

"Voices? Voices again, Tess?"

"Yes. Real ones, not imaginary. But the room was empty—so I went in to see—"

She saw his expression change; his body seemed to narrow, to fold in upon itself; on guard against her as though he were vulnerable before an enemy.

"So you went in to see where the voices came from?"

"I found the tape-recorder, Johnnie. I heard you and Olivia talking." She kept it up, that cool courage, in front of him!

"Well, and how much wiser are you for that bit of snooping?"

"I heard what you said, what Olivia said—"

He stood there rubbing his hands as though the blood were drained from them. She watched that intent and whitened face and knew that he was working out a method for dealing with her and her discovery.

"What you heard was very harmless, wasn't it? Olivia told me about the Chinese vase."

"I heard *all* the conversation—the end as well as the beginning." She could scarcely recognize her own quiet, relentless voice.

"Oh, I see! *That's* what's upsetting you! You're jealous! You heard that Olivia likes me a little too much. Well, what of it? I can't help women finding me attractive. Why mind? After all, it's you I married!"

"I'm beginning to wonder why!"

"Love seldom has a logical explanation." He was almost himself again, speaking lightly.

"Love? Did you ever love me, Johnnie?"

"What a question to ask! I don't know what to do about you, Tess. You worry me!"

"Then let me stop worrying you! Send me back home," she cried.

"Home?"

"England."

His mood changed again.

"You must know you're asking something quite impossible! You will stay here as long as I do! Perhaps it will be for years—"

"*No!*"

"But yes! I've got to keep an eye on you, Tess! And I couldn't if you were all that way away."

"You talk as though I needed a keeper!"

"Well—when you behave as you are doing now—"

"You can't *make* me stay here, Johnnie! I'm not a prisoner!"

"You're dependent upon me. How do you think you will get back to England on your own, without money? Fly by jet? Book a

110

luxury suite on a ship? Sorry, Tess, but I'm afraid your place is here. While Uncle Luke is alive, I shall never let you go! Did you hear that? *I shall never let you go!*"

Tess put out her hands and pushed against him with all her force. Taken unaware, he staggered back a little and she tore past him to the front door, opened it and slammed it behind her.

It was snowing hard and she had forgotten her snow boots. For a moment she stood hesitating, knowing how foolish it was to go anywhere in Canada without them, but no sense of her own discomfort could drag her back to the house to get them, she would rather suffer icy feet than risk being stopped by Johnnie.

As she began to run with difficulty up the drive, the snow, rutted by the family's parked cars, brushed icily against her ankles. Large flakes fell on her face, on her eyelids—she had never seen them dance before her so large, so soft and so deadly, as though they were her enemies trying to stop her flight from the house.

She couldn't see where she was going and, stumbling a little, felt two hands reach out of that blinding whiteness and catch hold of her, blocking her escape.

She cried out in alarm, wrenching herself away from the grip, and as she did so she stumbled. Her captor held her for a moment without speaking, letting her struggle.

"Let me go!" she almost shouted, dreading to look up and find Johnnie's narrow, mocking face. *"Let, me go . . . !"*

VIII

TESS BLINKED, looked up and took a breath of sheer relief.

"Oh Angus, *you!*"

"That's the second time," he said, "that you've nearly winded me! You're making quite a habit of it!" He was laughing, his voice was light but the grip on her arm was firm as though he felt her fear and wanted to reassure her.

"Where are you off to?"

"Anywhere," she cried a little wildly. "Downtown, uptown—I don't know!"

"Then come and have coffee with me. I was going to do some more work on your uncle's library, but that can wait." He looked down at her feet. "Where are your overshoes?"

"I don't need them. These have very thick soles—"

"You don't walk about Canada in winter in the kind of shoes you'd wear in England! Run and get them."

"No!" Her voice had a high, sharp note. "I'm all right, I tell you! I won't go back!"

"Very well, but I'd hate you to freeze."

She began to laugh as though he had said something funny and felt Angus' grip tighten and hurt her as though he sensed that she might be on the verge of hysteria. She pulled herself together.

"My car is just along the street," he said. "There were too many in your drive already— all large and opulent and expensive!" His tone was light, as though he were deliberately trying to ease her tension.

At the gateway, Tess looked back and thought she could see a face at the hall window. Johnnie watching her meet Angus? She was past caring. Walking along the street to his car, she faced the prospect of explanations when she reached home. Well, she had a weapon now—all she need do was to mention the tape-recorder. A weapon against her own husband . . . !

"You must excuse my dirty car." Angus was regarding it ruefully. "I got caught in a rutted road yesterday."

She waited, hoping he'd say he went to see friends, name them, and so assure her that there was no mystery about him, no shadow on his integrity.

"I've hired this Chrysler for my stay in Toronto," he went on. "It looked so nice when I first had it, but it's a work of art to keep a car looking like new in our Canadian winters."

She was only half listening, she had gone back to thoughts of Johnnie, wondering what would happen if she was ever goaded to tell someone—old Ginevra, for instance, about the tape-recorder, But, by that time, Johnnie would see to it there would be no evidence to support her story, and he would have his own terrible explanation. . . .

"Oh poor Tess! I hoped I'd never have to tell you! She's been ill. She has blackouts and hallucinations—she imagines things. That night she got here, for instance, and thought she heard someone . . . The doctors know about her—" Johnnie's charming, open face would look distressed and they would listen and believe him! Six months ago if anyone had told her that Johnnie would use the result of that car accident as a weapon against her, she would have thought it ludicrous. Now it was a fact, horrifying and almost limitless in its possibilities.

Tess got into the car as Angus opened the door for her. She settled down in her seat, trying to hold back the shivering that had not left her since she ran from the house. Angus

115

got in behind the driving wheel and switched on the heater.

She looked back once as they drove up the beautiful avenue of great houses. No one was following. What was the matter with her that she had to look back in fear? Anyone would think she was playing at melodrama. But try as she might, she couldn't laugh at herself. When this brief interlude with Angus was over, she would have to go back—and Johnnie would be waiting for her. . . .

They went to a small, pleasant hotel and Tess was grateful that the semicircular lounge was only dimly lit and that Angus chose a corner table. A niche with a mirror on one wall and a mass of indoor plants making an oasis of green on the other, gave a sense of seclusion.

Angus offered her a cigarette, then leaning back in his chair, he said quietly, his face turned away from her:

"I'm not going to pester you, Tess, but sometimes an outsider can help. I'll try if you want me to."

"Thank you," she said in a small, bleak voice, "but it's one of those problems that no-body can do anything about except the people concerned."

"I'm sure you're right—if it's just a matter

of being unhappy. But when a woman is really frightened—and you *were,* you know!—then I think it becomes something far more than just her personal domestic problem."

"It was stupid of me to be scared—there was no reason at all! It was just my own wretched imagination! I'm all right now!" She had roused herself to a semblance of over-bright assertion and waited for him to show reassurance. But he just sat back quietly, looking ahead of him, and said nothing.

"I suppose it's all the strangeness of a new country and new ways of living among strangers. You know—" she rushed on still in that high unnatural tone, "people don't realize how difficult adjustment is—" There was a pause. Then:

"Baloney!" said Angus. "That isn't the way to talk yourself out of being frightened, Tess! This isn't a primitive country with strange rites and hoodoos and tribal dances! This is *Canada*—modern, bustling, uninhibited Canada!" He watched the cigarette burning in his steady fingers. "But that doesn't mean to say that odd things don't take place in isolated establishments here—I guess odd things could happen in heaven! Angels could play 'ghosts' and harps could twang without hands!" He turned his head slightly and looked at her.

117

"Something odd took place in that house when you arrived—we both know that. All right! It was a housebreaker—or was it?"

"It must have been."

"Very well, we'll agree on that for want of a better explanation, but it doesn't explain the atmosphere."

She knew that Angus was aware of her quick turn of the head, her startled, "You feel it, too?"

"I know! I'm a stranger; you belong there, and I have no right to be saying what I am and you, in loyalty, should tell me to mind my own business. I would have done if I hadn't seen your frightened face as you ran down the drive. Tess, whether you feel I should discuss it or not, I'm going to tell you that someone in that house is walking on tiptoe, someone is creating an atmosphere of caution, of watchfulness—"

"Who? And why?"

He shook his head.

"Then, why are you telling me?"

"Because you were frightened and I wanted you to know that I sense something too!"

The waiter set the coffee and cream and sugar on the little glass table. Tess sat watching the young man's hands setting down the cups and thinking that if someone sensi-

118

tive caught the atmosphere of the house in Savernake Avenue at all, that was probably just how he would feel it—as though someone walked on tiptoe. . . .

It was later, when they were drinking their coffee, that the thought came to her that she had asked two questions in one. She had said: "Who? Why?" And Angus had only answered the latter. Did he know *who* it was who walked on tiptoe for some mysterious reason of their own? But how could he? Come to that, did *she* know? Her first thought was that it was Johnnie, playing dangerous games, with his tape-recorder. But what of Olivia, the niece, hitherto unknown, from San Francisco? Or old Ginevra, watching them with her secret, hooded eyes?

Angus leaned forward and, without asking her, refilled her coffee cup. Then he pushed back his chair.

"I'm going to get some more cigarettes. I shan't be a minute."

He walked away from her, and she was grateful for these moments in which to do something to her face.

A touch of powder, a line drawn in lipstick, heavier than usual so that it was like a banner to flaunt with courage against her fear, Thank heaven for makeup!

Her over-reddened lips grinned wryly at her reflection.

With her compact back in her handbag, she composed her face and watched the distant figure of Angus at the kiosk. She wanted desperately to be able to look at him without doubt; or question "Who is this man?" She liked him too strongly, too instinctively to have her faith shattered—and yet she could not trust him.

His name was not on the medical list of Vancouver doctors—yet he told them that he worked there. Everyone, it seemed, had taken him on trust—the friends of the Burnses, the Burnses themselves and now the uncle. Liking him, because that was his supreme art, to be liked and trusted? For what purpose did he practice it? Why had he come here? Why had he volunteered to work at a tedious job? If he was so interested in foreign travel he could get all the books he needed from a library; there was no need to work for nothing for a man he didn't know!

She watched him approach, threading his way through the tables. He sat down and laid a new packet of cigarettes on the table.

"English brand. You probably like them better than the American ones I smoke."

"Thank you." She met his gaze and smiled.

120

"That's better! You know"—he considered her—" when you smile your eyes crinkle up at the corners—"

"That means early wrinkles!"

"Oh, I shouldn't worry about that! People should have laughter lines—dead-pan faces never got anyone very far in life!" His hand rested on the table, his fingers were lean and strong, his nails well-kept.

Slowly, the hot coffee had done its work. She felt warm at last and slid out of her coat. Angus draped it over her chair.

The dim mirror on one wall gave her back her reflection; a slender girl with brushed-back hair that had chestnut lights in it, wearing a dark red sweater and a necklace of plain, twisted gold.

"Look, Tess, please don't mind my harping back on this! But just let me say one thing. You're in a strange country and it could be lonely, so if you should ever need help or advice, will you come to me?"

She knew the guard came down over her face. Her instinct still warned her that this man was a stranger and an impostor.

"Thank you, but—I'll be all right! I'm not one, anyway, to go running to someone for advice on—on little things! I've been brought up to fight my own battles. It's only that sometimes—"

"Sometimes," he said as her voice trailed off, "things get beyond you; they present problems mere common sense can't tackle. I know! That's why I ask you to remember, always, that an outsider's ear can possibly get a new slant on some seemingly hopeless angle. If I sound rather ponderous I'm sorry! What I really mean is this—" His hand touched her lightly and was immediately withdrawn. "If you should ever need me, need my help, wherever you are, I will come to you."

The words fell about her, filling the quiet corner space where they sat with vibrant feeling. Her blood quickened with the same strange excitement that she had felt when she stood with him in the study at the house on Savernake Avenue. Once again it was as though some strong magnetic force pulled her physically towards him.

"Don't be polite and say 'Thank you.' Don't say anything, Tess. Just remember that I mean every word of what I say."

"But why would you do this for me? Why come if—if I needed help? You scarcely know me!"

The soft light behind her chair caught his brilliant blue gaze.

"No, I suppose in a way I don't! And yet

sometimes one meets someone—you look across a room at a party; you are introduced in a restaurant or on a railway station—and straight away you know that you would never again meet as strangers! Nothing is felt between two people you know, Tess, that isn't felt at first sight! Even—friendship—"

"But I don't even know who you are." Impulse overcame caution. "I mean—your life—your work—?" her questions hung for a moment between them.

His blue gaze veered away from her, and although his voice was light when he answered her, his face was grave. "I've been wandering around the world. Soon I have to go back and take up my work again. In the meantime I'm here and I intend to stay for a little while—until what I have to do is finished."

"You mean the cataloguing of Uncle Luke's books?"

He hesitated. Then he said quietly:

"Yes, Tess, yes, of course—the cataloguing of your uncle's books."

But somehow she knew perfectly well that that was not what had been in his mind.

A thought struck her and before she stopped to think she voiced it.

"When we met on the train, I had an idea you were only passing through on your way back to

Vancouver. *Did* you intend, then, to stay in Toronto? Or did you only decide that when you met Uncle and he showed you his library?"

"I intended to stay."

"But you never dreamed you'd be meeting Uncle Luke, did you? Though you said you'd heard of him, you hadn't planned—"

He laid his hand over hers.

"You ask so many questions, Tess!" His eyes laughed.

"I'm sorry but—there's a lot I don't understand."

The laughter went from his face. It became closed and withdrawn. "Perhaps you never will! Perhaps I'm making a terrible mistake and I have no right to stay! But it's too late to do anything about it now! I think, if I'd met you earlier, I'd never have come to Toronto—"

"But what have *I* got to do with it?" she cried.

"So much more than you ever dream, Tess." He seemed visibly to pull himself together. "Would you like some more coffee?"

"No thank you." She reached for her coat.

"I've got an idea!" he said suddenly, glancing at his watch. "Were you going shopping?"

"Only to a little place on Bloor Street to buy a birthday present for a friend."

"That wouldn't take you long, would it?"

"No, but I was going to stay around for a while, just to look at the shops—"

"In other words, you didn't plan to get back for some time? Well, then, there are two hours before lunch—I don't suppose you eat much before one o'clock. Let's go out somewhere and look at the snow and get some sunshine."

"But—"

"Oh, Tess. Don't say 'No' when it could be such fun to say 'Yes'! I know a small country hotel not very far away which would be quite lovely this morning. We could go out there, have a bit of a walk and then come back well in time for you to do your one bit of shopping. Yes?"

"Well—"

"That's a fraction better than a 'But,' " he laughed, "but not good enough! Come on, Tess, steal two hours—just two small hours in a whole day! I won't forget that the shops close at one and I promise to bring you back in time for you to buy your birthday present."

"Suppose it's snowing? We wouldn't be able to go for a walk, would we?"

"Ah, but it isn't! When I went to the kiosk to get the cigarettes, I looked out of the door. The sun has come out and the sky is pure blue."

She was putting on her coat, arranging her scarf, picking up her gloves and bag from the chair next to her and taking a long time about it all. An hour or so away from the Bellairs house; away from Johnnie and Olivia and Ginevra. . . . For heaven's sake, all her life couldn't be lived in state of emotion! To drive with Angus out to some unknown place—to walk in peace for just a little while. . . .

Tess pushed back her chair.

"That's the girl!"

He laughed and pulled her to her feet. For a moment their gaze held; then he dropped her hands and said abruptly, "Come, Tess."

They drove through the busy Toronto streets and out into the country. It was a gay drive with Angus talking lightly, inconsequentially about all and everything except himself. He was a good companion and he could be amusing. Sitting by his side, hearing herself laugh, she wondered what old Luke would say if he knew, that she, a married woman, was driving into the country with another man! His narrow, bigoted code of behavior would be outraged. But Uncle Luke wouldn't know; nobody would! This was an hour or so stolen from her life in the Bellairs house, to be enjoyed, to be touched with laughter and inconsequence. An hour in which to be young, to be herself.

Angus began to sing:

"How many miles to Babylon?
Three score and ten—"

Tess joined in, with a kind of hit-or-miss at the tune.

"Can I get there by candle-light?
Yes, and back again."

Their voices rose above the purr of the car; the sun gleamed on the dark blue bonnet; over in the east a few ruffled clouds marched across the sky like the heads of old warriors. . . .

Tess was laughing over Angus' story of the first time he ever rode a camel, when they reached the Farraway Inn.

It was a long, low building with a wide porch running full length. There were gardens with every living thing in it sleeping under the snow, and beyond there was a wood thin and gleaming like a fairy forest in a pantomime.

Angus parked the car.

"I thought we'd go for a walk first and then come back and have a drink. Would you like that?"

"I'd love it."

He glanced doubtfully down at her shoes.

"The path through the wood is always swept of snow in winter because so many people come out either for the walk or because it's a shortcut to a lake where there's a lot of weekend skating, so I don't think you'll get wet."

"I'll get wet through and I won't care!" she cried, and felt that the shining white morning and the crystal air and Angus had gone to her head.

It was very still and isolated in the woods because most people were busy with weekend shopping. They walked side by side, not talking very much, keeping to the cleared path, slipping a little where ice was forming, and laughing as it cracked and they reached out to steady one another. Nothing was real to Tess except these moments; there was no past and no future. She lived and felt vibrant and young; the cold air stung her face; the trees made royal blue shadows on the snow. They met a big brown dog with a tail that waved like a windmill; they threw stones on to the frozen stream and watched them skid like pigmy skaters. Tess said she would like to see bears and Angus told her she'd have to go a long way west for those, but he'd make her a snow bear if she liked with pebbles for eyes and chips of ice for claws.

They talked, they laughed and sometimes lapsed into silence. If she told anyone about it, they'd say, "Oh, yes, a nice walk in the country." And they wouldn't know, and she could never explain, the quality of magic about it. Was it just reaction from the emotional strain at the house on Savernake Avenue? Was it mere contrast that turned this hour into an enchantment? If her life had been happy, would she look on this interlude with Angus as magic? She knew without a doubt, as she walked by his side, that whatever had gone before, there was something about this walk in the winter woods with a comparative stranger that set it on a level above all ordinary hours.

She ignored the small nagging warning that it would be dangerous to analyze it. She should just accept the moment, be grateful for it and then, when it was all over, push it back in her memory. She tried honestly to bring herself down to practical level. She was walking along a path in the woods; there was no witty conversation, no romantic excitement and yet there *was* the magic. . . .

And suddenly Tess knew the truth and therefore the danger.

I could love this man. . . .

But she had loved Johnnie and where was all that feeling now? This was nothing but reaction from fear and despair; nothing but imagination playing tricks. *Be your age, Tess*

Bellairs—this can't be love . . .!

She turned her head and at the same moment Angus looked at her. His eyes darkened and deepened and for a second his footsteps faltered. He seemed about to say something, he *did* say something, but it was obviously not what was first in his mind.

"Where's our pal, the brown dog?" and his dark blue eyes left her face to look about him for the mongrel.

Tess stood quite still. Her whole being trembled, for it was as though fate had in that crucial moment of her thoughts forced Angus to pause and look at her. She had her answer to her own self-mockery. *Be your age, Tess Bellairs! This can't be love.* It was, and a denial was merely a betrayal of her deepest self.

She realized that Angus was speaking.

". . . and so I think we'd better turn back. Your shoes must be wet, and you need a warm drink."

Ordinary words, practical in their suggestion! Deliberately so? For surely, as she had looked at Angus, something of her feeling had stolen out of her heart to shine in her eyes. . . .

She said, pointing:

"Oh look, there's the brown dog, through the trees, and he's got snow on his nose!" Her laughter was forced and unnatural but Angus gave no sign that he thought it so.

"They sometimes use big dogs like him to pull small sleds out on the prairies," he said. "I've seen them. One I know meets every train on the Vancouver run and gets a bone from the kitchen. He's quite a character. Come on, Tess." He glanced at her. "I'll race you to that clearing! One, two, *three*—"

They were off. Breathless, laughing, the moment of tension past, she flew after him. The dog joined the fun, leaping and barking, his tail weaving like drunken windmill shafts.

And then, in the bar of the Farraway Inn, Angus ordered Tess a sloe gin and dared her to say she didn't like it.

She said, "It's good!" and felt it slide down her throat like a warming flame.

The brown dog came too and wolfed cocktail biscuits.

Angus looked at Tess as they sat on the high stools, with the barman in the far corner, putting a coin in the jukebox as though he felt everyone wanted music.

"Thank you, Tess," Angus said, "for a lovely interlude."

"It was lovely for me, too!"

"Dear Tess!"

Dear Tess! She looked down at her glass. If he would say, "I want to go somewhere and kiss the breath out of you. . . ." Her heart turned over at the thought. *Stop it!* You're married to Johnnie, for better or worse—and heaven alone knew what the ultimate "worse" would be!

It took them twenty minutes to reach Toronto again and Angus set her down at the shop on Bloor Street where the statuette stood in the window along with an ebony cat and a little Japanese garden on a carved wood plinth.

"Will you promise me something?"

"What?"

They were standing by the open door of the car. "Promise that you will never forget that you aren't entirely alone out here: that, as I said, if you want me, I will come to you."

As though, she thought shakenly, she had no husband, no man to stand with her against anything that might happen. . . . She believed that she nodded her head.

Angus seemed satisfied for he said "Good-bye," and got back quickly into the car. A small boy, clutching his load of newspapers, shot past to his pitch by a street standard and nearly knocked her over.

Tess crossed the sidewalk and paused for a moment looking into the shop window. She wasn't entirely alone because a stranger was prepared to come to her if she called to him . . . a man with Viking-blue eyes . . . a man in a masquerader's cloak . . . Angus Dalzell who called himself a doctor, from a city where his name was not known. . . .

Think hardly of him; mistrust him! Tell yourself that he's an adventurer and you're just a little fool who doesn't know what his game is! All right, go on, Tess Bellairs, tell yourself all these things—and then stop loving him!

She shivered and pulled her fur collar up around her throat. With the newspaper boy's piercing untranslatable shout "Globe-n-Mail" she walked into the shop to buy Sally's birthday present.

IX

It was quarter to one when Tess reached the house again. The three cars had been put away in the enormous garage and she walked up the cleared drive.

When she let herself in, she found no one in the hall. For a moment she stood against the closed door and looked about her. Flowers glowed from the great blue bowl on the long table; the pictures—two originals of Canadian scenes, one entrancing street scene by old Grandma Moses—caught the light from the tall windows. Uncle Luke's beautiful Chinese embroidered screen still stood in the corner waiting for Ginevra to do a little more repair work on it. A gracious and charming hall, almost palatial, with the staircase curving upwards to the first wide landing where the oriel window flung down a blaze of stained glass color. A house to be lived in with happiness!

134

"Hallo Tess—"

She started and turned her head.

"Hallo Johnnie."

He was standing in the doorway of the little sitting-room and there was no escape.

"There's nearly ten minutes to go before lunchtime. Come in here; I want to talk to you."

"I must take my things off and change my shoes—" she began. But Johnnie stood waiting and she crossed the hall, silent and obedient as a child, knowing that she could not avoid whatever punishment he had thought up for her.

"What have you been buying?" Johnnie moved into the room with her and pushed the door to.

"A present for Sally."

"I never could resist brown paper packages!" His tone was friendly, his manner almost jaunty.

"Undo it and let me see," he began and when she hesitated, he coaxed: "Show! Show Johnnie!"

Her hands trembled a little as she undid the parcel. She suspected this sudden reversion to friendliness. She felt him reach up and draw her coat from her shoulders, and slid her arms out of the sleeves carefully so that she should not feel the touch of his hands. He tossed the coat on to a chair and watched her open the white box, that held the statuette.

"Why, it's charming!" He took it and held it in his hands.

"I got it because Sally loves cats."

"Does she? One of these days we'll have to go down to the States and you must introduce me."

She did not answer.

Johnnie laid the little statuette back in the box.

"Women love gee-gaws," he said musingly, "and men like gadgets! Like my tape-recorder—a grown-up's toy! Uncle Luke paid me my commission on some land I'd sold up at Chillawoka and I bought the machine. I may have played about a bit with jobs, but my training has been in engineering, so"—he opened a white jade cigarette box on the table—"well, when I got it home, I couldn't resist experimenting. I was interested to find out how much the recorder would pick up from a distance. That's why I got that idea of fixing it up in the chimney."

Tess stood quietly listening, tense and on guard, her fingers playing with the string that had tied the parcel.

"There's a point in the chimney," Johnnie went on, watching her, "where it connects with the one downstairs in the study. This house is old by Canadian standards and I believe that at some time or other in the history of the house, some primitive form of heating the two rooms by a connecting pipe carried up through the chimney must have been tried. Well, so I had fun seeing how inventive I could be. You know the rest."

She should have said nothing, have left the matter there. But, for the life of her, she couldn't. Johnnie's facile explanation was straining too much at her intelligence!

"If it was so innocent," she said, watching her fingers weave in and out of the knotted string, "why were you angry when I overheard Uncle Luke's voice coming from your room?"

"Oh, that's the small boy in me, Tess!" His smile was disarming. "You'll have to understand that all men have a bit of them that has never grown up! You know how kids like to find hide-outs—to have their secret games, safe from grown-up interference? Well, that tape-recorder and my discovery that I could use it to listen in downstairs—was my small boy secret!"

"You, don't expect to keep the fact that you've got a tape-recorder a secret in this house, do you?"

"Good heavens, no! Aunt Ginevra saw me

bring it in. She wasn't very much interested. She said it was a waste of money buying it because there was already one somewhere in the house. She said it had been a nine days' wonder and it was probably somewhere up in the attic."

"And you decided that to record private conversations was just an innocent pastime!"

"For Pete's sake, I only listened in to Uncle Luke talking to Cosmo Rankin! Well, and why not? If we take another view of the whole matter, why *shouldn't* I know what's going on?"

"When a man shuts himself in his study with his lawyer it's because he wants a very private talk and not one recorded on some eavesdropper's reel of tape!"

She was surprised that her voice was so calm, implying such a complete, and false, command of herself.

"Oh, Tess." Johnnie's voice had become soft again. "What a dangerously suspicious little person you are! This way of yours of jumping to damaging conclusions—"

"Not jumping, Johnnie! Just having them forced upon me."

"But look here, don't you see? I can erase the whole of that conversation from the tape!"

"When you've thoroughly digested all that's on it?"

She had said too much. She knew it, but she didn't flinch when his hand shot out and caught her face with a sharp blow.

"If you do that again, Johnnie," she said very quietly. "I shall go to Uncle Luke and ask him to lend me the money to go back to England. And if he refuses unless I tell him why I'm leaving you, then I *shall* tell him."

"Threats?"

"Yes."

"But I *won't* be threatened—"

"So we both know where we are!"

Their eyes met, cold with antagonism—eyes that had once looked at one another with tenderness, had laughed and closed under the sweet delight of loving. . . .

Tess turned away, feeling sick, aware of her left cheek still stinging under the vicious swing of his hand.

"So there's nothing you can tell against me," Johnnie was saying. "If you went to Uncle Luke with such a silly story, well—I'd have to tell him about that breakdown of yours, wouldn't I? I'll have to say: 'Tess is unbalanced. She's making up stories about me.' I'd also have to tell him that you worked it very nicely to have Angus Dalzell in the house, Tess! But today you did a brash thing and spoilt it all for yourself. You had him

139

come to fetch you and take you out this morning. Now, to get down to today's escapade. *Where did you two go?*" His voice lost its menacing softness and rasped.

He tried to force her to meet his eyes but she kept hers averted.

"Angus was coming in to do some more work in Uncle Luke's library this morning. I met him in the drive and we went together and had some coffee. It was a spur of the moment decision."

"You took an unconscionable long time to have your coffee."

"I went shopping as well. I was determined to stay out until lunchtime—and *you* know why."

"You would be playing a dangerous game, my sweet, to get involved with Dalzell. For one thing, I'm suspicious of him, and so is Olivia. For another—"

"For another," she cried, "I'm your wife. I know! But I'm not a prisoner, Johnnie; you can't keep me if I choose to go—"

She saw a flicker of uncertainty in his eyes, as though he knew he hadn't broken her spirit. His voice changed, cajoled.

"Look, Tess, I'll tell you everything. Perhaps then you'll understand. I *did* want to hear what Uncle Luke had to say to the lawyer.

After all, he sent for me to come out and I gave up my job. I've been here over two months and I want to know if I'm wasting my time. He won't tell me anything—he likes to keep Olivia and me guessing. After all, there's no guarantee that he won't leave his money in the end to some deserving cause and then all this time I've spent out here will have been wasted. There's nothing wrong in wanting to know—it's Uncle Luke who's being unfair! What *I* did was merely practical, Tess. I had a right to know where I stood."

"You could have gone to Uncle Luke and had a quiet word with him and asked him if there were any prospects—say—for you to enter his firm. Put like that, he couldn't object."

"He's tricky! And, like lots of men who have made a fortune from nothing, he's suspicious where money is concerned. The way I did it, I've learned a lot more than he'd ever have told me. Shall I tell you what I know, Tess?"

"It doesn't matter."

"Oh, but it does! You're in this as much as I am! As it stands at the moment, Olivia and I share three quarters of his fortune, the rest goes to some hospital out near Calgary. Ours will be a sizable sum, Tess. I heard him tell Rankin how he wanted the will drawn up. I heard him say that he was pleased with me; he thinks I'm a nice chap—and you're 'the sort of wife I'd have liked Johnnie to have!' So you see, *you* come into it, too! One day I'll be a rich man—"

"And—and Olivia—will be—a rich—woman—"

The smile froze from his face.

"Could there be some hidden meaning in that remark?"

"You forget I heard almost all of that conversation between you and Olivia down in Uncle Luke's study. I heard Olivia say: 'Half isn't as good as the lot . . . the whole lovely lot!' "

"Well—she's right, of course. She'd like to get her hands on my share, too! I guess that's what she meant; I don't know."

"You *do*, Johnnie. You said: 'You should burn as a witch!' You grasped her meaning and it didn't displease you! In fact I believe you were laughing when you said it."

"Stop it! Stop, do you hear?" Johnnie's anger broke about her. "Everything you say is just another pointer to your unbalanced state. Get this into your pretty muddled head. Olivia is a cousin; *you* are my wife and if you're trying to work it so that you can get free of me, then I warn you, don't. Nothing and nobody is going to part us—not while Uncle Luke is alive! He'd never condone a

142

broken marriage."

"If—" she cried, "if I'm unbalanced and hysterical, as you're trying to suggest, he would feel differently. He'd understand if we couldn't live together."

"Oh no! I'm the husband who looks after my young wife!" His eyes were narrowed in a knowing derision.

"I could go back to England," she said wildly, "and you could tell Uncle Luke what story you liked. I wouldn't care. I'd be away from it all!"

He shook his head. "I shall behave with admirable devotion towards you. I shall be long-suffering and cheerful in my terrible adversity. I shall say: 'She can't help behaving as she does, you see it's a sickness—' " His eyes were narrowed still with that knowing derision. "So, Tess, I don't think you'll tell anyone how I used the tape-recorder because it'll be your word against mine, and then I'd have to tell Uncle Luke about that terrible experience you had which affected your—er—mental health—"

Curiously, the words, the threats had lost their impact. She felt suddenly only a deep, terrible regret that she had ever believed she loved him.

"This house has done something to you,

Johnnie. This house—or—the money it stands for. I don't understand how anyone can change so terribly. Or *have* you changed? Did I ever know you? Is that it?"

"For heaven's sake! Who really knows who in this world?"

"For once," she said, "you've spoken the truth!"

In the hall, Madrigal was hammering the gong as though she were a drum-major gone berserk.

"Run along and do your face, Tess. You look a bit like a ghost."

She turned from him without speaking, the box with the little statuette in her arms.

Upstairs in the bedroom she stared at her reflection in the gilded mirror. So much said, and nothing conclusive! Just hints and threats and fear lying over her like a cloud.

I've got to get away. But, without money or friends here to help, how could she? Johnnie had said again: "While Uncle Luke is alive, I shall never let you go." But when he died, what would Johnnie do? Pay her off, get rid of her and marry Olivia? Join their fortunes?

"You should burn for a witch!" . . . A witch like Circe who had enchanted men . . . the girl from San Francisco with the raven hair, who had cried softly, "Johnnie! Johnnie, darling—"

144

"Tess, lunch is ready," Ginevra was calling her.

"I'm just coming—"

She pulled herself together, did her face and brushed her hair back smoothing it to the shape of her head. Then she sat for a moment.

She knew now that through all that sinister conversation with Johnnie, thought of Angus had fortified her. . . . Suppose she went to him and told him everything; asked him what she should do?

And, as the thought came to her, it was as though she had conjured his image and he stood there, just behind her, looking at her face in the mirror, smiling at her. . . .

"Tess!" It was Johnnie who now called her.

She started up and ran from the room.

X

OVER LUNCH GINEVRA announced that she had that morning finished a mask she had been making of Johnnie.

"Me?" He sat up, waving a knife in the air like a small, startled boy. "But how can you? I only sat for you once! You said you wanted quite a number of sittings because you like to study your sitter, and I haven't had time—"

The large lids came down like shutters over her eyes, her long, narrow mouth smiled.

"I've studied you plenty!" she said, "and I think it's a good likeness. The oil paint hasn't yet had time to dry, but this evening you can all come and see it."

"You'll have to make a mask of Tess," Luke said. "Then, when the family is complete, I suggest we have them on a dark screen in one of the rooms."

"To scare burglars!" Johnnie laughed.

Luke looked around the table with pleasure.

"It's good having you all here. Johnnie and now Tess. The next thing I want to see is you married, Olivia. You're twenty-six; it's time you found yourself a husband among your admirers."

Olivia raised her eyes and looked at the old man at the head of the table.

"Oh, I'll marry, Uncle Luke! Don't worry! I'll find just the husband I want—but in my own good time. There's no hurry!" Her eyes moved for a flash of an instant to Johnnie.

Tess saw, and something made her glance towards Ginevra. She was quietly breaking the crisp brown roll on the beautiful pure white Meisson side-plate, her eyes down. But Tess knew that she had been perfectly aware of that glance between Olivia and Johnnie as though some ancient witch at her christening had given her second-sight. What else did she know? And, of what she knew, would she ever tell?

Olivia helped herself to salad and her small green stone earrings glittered.

"By the way"—Luke tackled his laden plate—"I expected Dalzell around this morning. I wanted to talk to him about the arrangement of the books on the shelves."

Johnnie looked across the table at Tess and raised his eyebrows. Nobody spoke.

147

"Well?" the old man demanded. "Has anyone seen him?"

"I have—" Tess began.

"Did he say why he didn't turn up this morning?"

"Tess ran into him in the town." Johnnie spoke before she could answer. "Didn't you, sweet?"

"And you know, Uncle, the poor chap must have *some* time to himself! You're not paying him for this job he's taken on."

The old man bridled and then grinned. "You're right, son!"

"It's a good thing you've got me here to keep you from cracking the whip too often! Fine thing when a young man has to keep his senior in order! You're an old dictator, Uncle Luke!" He said it with such affection, such charm, and Luke sat, seeming to preen himself in it. Johnnie was a son-of-a-gun, a young Adonis, a charmer, and, as far as the old man could love anyone but himself, he adored him.

He turned to Ginevra.

"Ring Dalzell at his hotel after lunch and ask him to dinner tonight. If he can't come, ask him for Thursday."

It was late afternoon and nearly dark when Tess went into the sunroom to look through some gramophone records piled there.

Ginevra came out of her studio, saw Tess and opened the sunroom door. She was rubbing her long, thin hands together.

"I've just put the mask on the screen," she said.

"You're pleased with it?"

She nodded. "It's Johnnie. You'll see!" she said enigmatically. And then she glanced out of the window. "It's been freezing all day and it's colder than ever tonight. There are icicles over the back door that'll have to be cleared away tomorrow. If you want to put the gramophone on, Tess, why don't you get Johnnie to take it into the small sitting-room, it's more comfortable than this room in winter."

"I only want to hear a couple of records, Aunt Ginevra."

"All right! But close the shutters over the windows; it'll make the room seem warmer. Oh, and by the way, Angus was out when I rang so I left a message. As he hasn't called back, I suppose he's coming tonight. I gave Thursday as an alternative date in my message and asked him to ring if he couldn't manage today."

When she had gone, Tess curled up on one of the long, low brightly-colored seats and listened to Schubert's songs. Darkness fell outside and she sat and looked out at the stars so

149

low in the sky that it was as though one could reach up and pick them like silver flowers.

It was peaceful in here with just the music and the soft darkness and, without a light, she put on whatever record she found next. One was a long-playing record of Beethoven's Pastoral Symphony. The music swelled through the room and, enchanted, she lost count of time.

When the symphony ended she took the record off and closed the gramophone. As she turned away she saw a shadow pass the windows. It was too dark to recognize the figure, but nobody had used the back door while she had been in the sunroom. Perhaps some boys were playing tricks on each other, hiding around houses. But they didn't do that in this elegant, dignified street! A tradesman? But he'd ring the back doorbell. Somebody then had quietly encircled the house. *I'm making a mystery of something that's probably perfectly reasonable,* she thought, going out of the sunroom. But as she went through the green baize door and into the hall, she heard a sound and a white envelope slid through the letter box. So whoever she had seen had merely come to deliver a letter. But in that case, why encircle the house? Why not just come to the front door?

She went to pick the envelope up and saw

that it was addressed to Ginevra. She opened the living-room door and handed it to the old lady.

"Now, whose writing is that?" She peered at the envelope.

Tess said nothing. She went out of the room and found to her relief that Johnnie wasn't in the bedroom. These days she shrank from being alone with him; from the Judas-intimacy of his look or his touch. . . .

She changed quickly into the gray, watered silk dress she had brought out from England, because Luke liked to show the women of his family off to visitors and tonight Angus was coming.

She wanted desperately to see him again, to hear his voice, to feel his eyes resting with kindness upon her. She hung about the room, prolonging the choice of a necklace or a brooch from her small collection of jewelry, not wanting to go down among them till Angus came. Then the clock struck seven and she wondered if she had missed his arrival.

Luke, Olivia and Johnnie were in the living-room and as Tess entered, Ginevra came closer on her heels.

"Dinner's almost ready—"

"We'll have to wait for Dalzell."

"Oh, but he's not coming. Didn't I tell you?"

"You did not!"

"Tess found a letter from him on the mat. I'm sorry, Luke, I quite forgot to tell you."

"You people with durned artistic temperaments!" he grumbled. "Where'd you be if it weren't for folks like us who keep our heads and our memories? You're like Mother, Ginevra, she was cuckoo-brained!"

The woman's strange old eyes flashed with sudden anger.

"You haven't had to wait for your meal, if that's what's worrying you!" she snapped.

"I'm just wondering what next you'll forget. First it was the back door that night Tess arrived—"

"I told you, Uncle," Olivia interrupted, "Aunt Ginevra locked that door. And maybe nobody broke in, anyway; maybe Tess only *thought* she heard someone—"

"Dalzell heard something, too—"

Olivia smiled with a faint, secret knowingness. "He could have just been humoring her because she was nervous."

"Someone"—Tess spoke up—"*was* in this house when I arrived. You can think it imagination on my part if you like but that doesn't alter the fact—" she broke off. She had been watching Luke and she saw his gaze, with a flicker of something almost like amusement, flash to Johnnie and she guessed that Johnnie had persuaded his uncle that it had been Tess' heightened imagination. *He's paving the way very quietly and thoroughly,* she thought, *to explaining away anything that I might do to incriminate him.* At that moment Johnnie flashed a smile at her—open and kind and friendly. *He's my husband, and my enemy! What is it in this house that has so changed him? Or was he never what I thought him?*

"When's Dalzell coming, did he say?"

"Yes, he has accepted the alternative date, Thursday," Ginevra said. "He said in his note that our line is out of order, so he couldn't get through on the telephone."

After dinner, they were going in to see the mask.

"Put on your coats," Luke said. "You'll get chilled even going those few paces from the house to the studio."

Olivia flung her beaver around her shoulders and a subtle scent of sandalwood broke about Tess from the satin lining.

Ginevra and the men had moved down through the baize door. Olivia said softly:

"Did you have a good time this morning with Angus?"

"I had a nice hot cup of coffee—"

"Really? And did you find out just who he is?"

"I didn't ask him about himself. He's a doctor and some friends of Sally's in the States know him—I've told you that."

"Yes, you have. And somebody is fooling someone, you know!"

"What do you mean?"

"Your dear Angus Dalzell is no doctor, nor does he come from Vancouver. He's an imposter—oh, a very charming one, I grant you. But then they always are—"

"How did you find out—about his not being a doctor?"

"I have ways!" Her tawny gold eyes snapped. "I don't take people on trust. Nor would Uncle Luke if he weren't in his dotage."

"He couldn't control a great business if he'd reached that stage!"

"Then he's just sentimental about people who've been to places where he's been! Ruthless people are very often sentimental, you know. It goes together—the tycoon who can weep over the death of a wife he neglected in life; the store magnate who can overwork his staff and break down when he sees a lost puppy. That's Uncle Luke! Fooled over a man who can talk to him about Katmandu and elephants!"

"If you think Angus an imposter, why don't you tell Uncle Luke so?"

"Oh I shall, but in my own good time. I want to see the fun first! I'm not spoiling the whole interesting episode for the sake of a few weeks! You know the saying about giving a man enough rope and he'll hang himself? Well, you'll be in at the kill, too, dear!" Her mouth was smiling and cruel. "The hounds will get him in the end, your dear Angus Dalzell—your phony doctor!"

But Tess had pushed open the green baize door and it swung behind her.

She reached the studio just as Luke, feet apart, stared at the black screen standing in pride of place in the center of the room.

"Godalmighty!"

"For Pete's sake!"

"What's happened? Oh no—*no!*"

The onslaught of voices rang around Tess. The screen was just a wall of unbroken black. On the floor below lay the mask, slashed to pieces.

"Perhaps it fell—" Olivia's words came from somewhere behind Tess.

"It was firmly secured to the screen. Besides, if it fell it wouldn't break like that!"

"What are you getting at?" Luke demanded. "That it was purposely done?"

"Yes," Ginevra said without turning around.

"But for the love of Jehovah, why?"

"Perhaps someone doesn't like me!" Johnnie said with a faint laugh.

Ginevra went forward and stirred the pieces with her foot.

"It was quite intact this afternoon."

But a little later, someone had slipped past the sunroom windows. And in only the time it took to skirt the house, Tess had reached the hall and had seen a white envelope fall softly on to the mat. Angus' acceptance of the invitation to dinner for Thursday night!

But Angus would have no reason for destroying the mask even if he knew about it, or had been in the studio for some other reason and seen it. Or could the mask have been slashed by accident? It seemed unlikely—it seemed such a senseless act of destruction. . . .

"I see things in faces," Ginevra had said. Things that other people didn't, and she put those hidden characteristics, that essence, into her work for others to see. The mask that was the reality, the face that was the mask. . . .

Tess was suddenly aware that Johnnie had turned around and was looking at her. She felt the blood rush to her face.

"I don't pretend to understand what seems a sort of perverted joke, but there's no point in staying in this ice-house," said Luke. "Well,

Ginevra, you'll have to start all over again."

He put his hand on her shoulder in an unexpectedly warm gesture. She looked suddenly very old, huddled in her beautiful coat.

"I'll make a bet it was some passing young hooligan," Luke was saying. "Come on out, all of you. Ginevra, you'd better lock your studio if you want your work intact."

"Perhaps," Olivia said flippantly, "there's a ghost in the house—one of the few ghosts in Canada! Tess heard footsteps in the dark, remember, the night she arrived. And now—this—"

And the other thing none of them dare mention in case Luke was hoaxing them all—the theft of the K'ang Hsi vase. Johnnie *could* have told his uncle about it and he could have laughed; have said, "It's a good joke, son! It's my secret! Of course it isn't genuine. But don't give me away!"

Johnnie was saying:

"I vote we all have some more coffee. I'm cold. Come, Tess, you heat some up for us."

The seemingly meaningless, futile destruction of the mask had cast a kind of macabre shadow and they felt it. They all said "Yes," they'd like some more coffee.

"I'll get the tray ready," Johnnie said. "It won't take five minutes."

157

They left Johnnie there in the kitchen with Tess. Immediately they had disappeared, Johnnie turned to her.

"Well? Why did you do it?"

"Do what?" She turned the electric switch under the percolator.

"Destroy that mask of me?"

It was so outrageous that there was no answer. She set the coffeepot more firmly on the gleaming cream stove.

"Tess, answer me!"

She swung around. "There is no answer! The question's ludicrous, and I'm going into the living-room with the others. You can make the coffee."

But it wasn't so easy. He held her shoulder and struggling would achieve nothing; experience had proved his strength to her.

"You were missing for a couple of hours late this afternoon, Tess. Aunt Ginevra said you were playing records in the sunroom—just three steps from the back door! Well? What mad, mischievous reason made you destroy that mask?"

"If you'll let go of my arm I'll go and ask Uncle Luke if yours is the general idea. If the others think I did it."

"You'll only make things bad for yourself. It would merely lead to an explanation—*my*—

158

explanation—"

His meaning was so simple—and so evil! This, too, could be held against her! One more thrust at the doubtfulness of her sanity! *"You see, this is the sort of malicious, meaningless thing Tess does! She doesn't know she's doing them—she has blackouts."*

Was this the reason why the mask had been destroyed—to point one more finger at her? And then she remembered again the dark shadow passing the sunroom window, the white envelope on the mat. There was no reason to circle the house in order to put something through the front-door letter box—no earthly reason! Whoever had been there had walked stealthily—

At that moment the telephone bell rang.

But, according to Angus, the telephone was out of order. Could it have been merely an excuse he had given in order to come to the house, unexpected and undisturbed in the dark?

But why? *Had* he been in Ginevra's studio? Again, why?

"Tess—" Olivia's voice called from the hall. "You're wanted on the telephone."

Tess wrenched herself away from Johnnie and fled.

Olivia stood in the hall, cool, poised, and

amused, watching her approach.

"Your phony doctor!" she said, and walked into the living-room.

Tess seized the receiver. "You want to speak to me, Angus?"

"Yes. Listen, Tess, I'm ringing to ask you if you left a scarf in the car. You didn't, but that's the ostensible reason why I rang up. Do you understand?"

"No," she said for anyone in the house to hear, "I don't think I left my scarf in your car, Angus."

"I had to know if you are all right."

"Quite all right. But Angus, you left a note to say you couldn't come and eat with us tonight and you said that the telephone was out of order."

"That's right, I did—"

"But—"

"I'm ringing off now. Remember what I told you this morning. Never, never forget it, Tess."

The telephone clicked and there was silence.

"Remember what I told you. Wherever you are, if you want me, I will come to you."

"So the phone's in order again now?"

She turned. "Yes, Johnnie."

"Who wanted you?"

"Angus, to ask if I had left a scarf in his car."

160

"Odd! I thought he found the telephone out of order!"

"It was."

"And Angus rang you about a scarf! Well! Well!" He rocked a little backwards and forwards, on heel and toe, watching her. "From what I've seen of your scarves they're pretty bright, neither of you could have missed it on the seat of the car or the floor when you got out. So, was it just an excuse to call you?"

Tess brushed past him without answering.

"And under cover of asking you if you'd left an imaginary scarf in the car, what did Angus want to know? Or to tell you?"

If it weren't for the fact that there was no extension in the kitchen, she would have thought Johnnie had been listening in. She said, keeping her voice calm:

"What *could* Angus tell me? *I* don't know! Do you?"

"Why don't you tell me the truth, instead of hedging?"

"Because there is absolutely nothing to tell."

"Little liar!" he whispered softly. "Come to the kitchen and get the coffee and tell me—"

She neither obeyed him nor justified herself against his mocking, whispered accusation. If he didn't believe her, then he didn't! But she would do anything rather than have another of these bitter, violent arguments.

She went into the living room, leaving Johnnie standing there in the great hall.

The family was sitting in a semicircle with Luke dominating the scene. She felt their eyes on her as she entered and sat down in one of the big chairs, composing herself and preparing to listen to their conversation.

Ginevra was talking about some new sun-blinds she was ordering and some lounging chairs from Denmark which she wanted for the garden.

"You spend my money too easily!" Luke snapped.

"If I didn't," she retorted, "you'd cause a crisis with your hoarding! If you don't mind people whispering between themselves as to whether you're as financially secure as you'd have them think, then fine! Go ahead and hoard. *I* don't care!"

"How a man lives has nothing to do with his financial status. I've known paupers who have lived for a while like millionaires and rich men who have looked like tramps—"

"All right," Ginevra retorted impatiently. "So we won't have the chairs or the awning or anything else for the garden! You're a mean man, Luke Bellairs. You'll die a miser!"

"Boloney!"

"You know quite well it isn't. People's idio-syncrasies tend to get exaggerated as they grow older. But don't worry, *I'll* buy the chairs."

"That you won't. It's my house. I'll buy them."

Ginevra's eyes closed and opened again. She looked across at her brother, smiling faintly. She knew how to deal with him, Tess thought. In her way, she was as strong-willed as he, though she was more subtle and far more discerning.

Olivia was saying:

"Can we have yellow chairs, Uncle Luke? It's such a heavenly color in the garden."

Her uncle answered her and the conversation milled around Tess. But she no longer troubled to listen. She let her mind go back to Angus.

He had admitted that he had said in his note that the telephone was out of order—but not that it actually was so. Again she wondered if he had merely wanted a chance to come in the dark and walk around the house. An excuse for being there if anyone saw him? But why? Why did people watch houses and probe and study them as Angus had seemed to be doing?

She sat there, with the conversation over chairs and awnings and wrought-iron garden tables swimming over her head, her mind absorbed in the problem and mystery of Angus Dalzell.

The house was full of Eastern treasures, perhaps these were a temptation, perhaps— she pushed her piling-up suspicions away. Angus was no criminal. . . . But he *was* an imposter—no argument could disprove that! Yet, helpless to control her wayward heart, she loved him. . . .

XI

Tess was suddenly aware of Luke saying:

"That call just now was for you, wasn't it?" His eyes were fastened on Tess.

"Yes."

"Olivia tells me it was Dalzell—"

Tess nodded.

". . . ringing you?"

"To ask if Id left a scarf in his car. We happened to meet and had a cup of coffee together."

"Who does he think he is, ringing another man's wife?" Luke's voice rose fiercely, his massive brows were drawn together. He looked, Tess thought, like a great, avenging Moses!

"I think it was a perfectly natural thing," she said, quick to Angus' defense. "After all, it was my scarf. He wouldn't be ringing anyone else about it, would he?"

There was a moment's pause while Luke lit one of his outsize cigars. Tess looked from one to the other. They were watching her, yet there was no flicker of affection, of warmth in any face. It was as though they were scenting trouble and were amused by it—Ginevra's strange old eyes conjectured; Olivia waited.

Luke puffed smoke into the room.

"If Dalzell is up to monkey tricks then he can stay away!"

Tess began to say, "I don't understand—" and then shut her mouth tight, because she knew perfectly well. This was Luke Bellairs in his puritan mood; this was the man who sang hymns at the top of his voice and called forth fire and damnation on human weaknesses.

"You're being old-fashioned, Uncle Luke," Olivia put in. "These days people think nothing of having friendships with the other sex after they're married. It's supposed to be modern and—er—quite harmless." Smiling and falsely gentle in her tone, she had successfully registered the impression that in Tess' case it wasn't harmless at all! "It's considered very out of date, Uncle, to spend the rest of your life going around with your husband," she added for full measure.

"I wasn't—" Tess broke in furiously. But Luke interrupted.

166

"However modern it's supposed to be, it won't be done here. Dalzell can find his own friends. Tess is Johnnie's wife—"

"If you'll let me speak—" she cried angrily.

"We'll say no more about it," the old man snapped his command. "Only, don't do it again."

"But I—" Tess began and then stopped. Very faintly she had seen Ginevra shake her head. It was as though in that moment, the strange, secretive old woman was on her side, and warning her not to continue the argument.

"About that mask," Luke was saying, "I'll ring the police. If hooliganism has started around here, then we'll want more protection. What are you shaking your head for, Ginevra?"

She said in her low, rasping voice, "The damage is done; if boys were trespassing here, they've been gone a long time now and the police won't be able to do anything. I'll lock my studio in future—"

"I've already spoken about having more patrols around these parts—I'll get on to them again tomorrow. I've got a fine garden; I'm not having gangs of kids uprooting bulbs—"

"They wouldn't—"

"Wouldn't they? Somebody entered this house while we were at the Club; somebody

167

slashed the mask you made. Well, what am I supposed to do? Wait till they burn my home down?"

"All right, Luke, *go* to the police."

"You're durned right I will!"

Johnnie, carrying in coffee, asked from the doorway:

"What's someone so darned right about?"

"That I'm going to the police."

Johnnie's eyes flicked to Tess. He set down the tray, saying, "Perhaps the mask did fall and get smashed."

"That wasn't a break caused by falling! A strong knife had been used."

"You make me feel very important." Johnnie perched on the arm of Ginevra's chair, watching her set out the gold and green coffee cups. "Going to the police because of me!"

"I'm going," snapped old Luke, "before some hooligan element in the town does far more serious damage here!"

"Oh." He grinned across at his uncle. "That deflates *me* and puts me in my place!"

This could be the moment to tell them that she had seen someone pass the sunroom window. But it would only call attention to herself and no one might believe her. What was the use, anyway, of saying that you had seen a dark shadow, that you didn't know

168

whether it was a man or a woman?

She wished she could pin the destruction on to Johnnie himself. Was it possible that he had done it, knowing that Ginevra fashioned the masks with uncanny insight into people's real characters, and that Luke might see, in that molded face, something that would check his delight in his long-lost nephew?

But Tess had been within sight of the back door for those two hours after Ginevra had come out of the studio and nobody else had passed in or out. And Johnnie had been in the living room with the family because she had heard his voice. . . .

"Tess, you're not drinking your coffee," Johnnie said, watching her with kindly concern. "Don't tell me I've made it too strong!"

"No."

"Darling, you look cold." His concern deepened. "That's standing around in the studio—"

"We're all cold through standing around in the studio," Olivia snapped.

"I turn off the heating when I'm not working in there."

"No need to waste it on a great empty room," said Uncle Luke.

Johnnie half rose. "I'll go and get you something to put around your shoulders, Tess."

"I don't want it." She heard the note of un-

169

graciousness in her voice and for the life of her could not smile at Johnnie or look grateful for his concern. This was just another act put on for Uncle Luke's benefit. Whatever she might do or be accused of doing, Johnnie's behavior should be exemplary—he was setting the pattern of an ideal husband.

On Monday Angus came around to work in the study and at eleven o'clock Tess decided to have her coffee with him.

For that first moment when he turned his head as she entered, Tess felt strongly that Angus was not pleased to see her. But he smiled at her, slid down from his perch on the ladder and said politely, "Hallo, Tess."

She refused to be disconcerted by that doubtful glance he had first flashed at her. "I've been typing lists of figures for Uncle Luke and I'm seeing numbers before my eyes! I won't interrupt you, Angus—at least, I'm afraid I will, but only for a minute or two."

He was leafing through a large beautiful book on Greece—she watched the rich colors of the illustrations flick through his fingers.

"Can I put a question to you first?" he asked.

"Of—of course—"

"Have you mentioned the K'ang Hsi vase to

anyone?"

"Yes, to Olivia. At first I didn't mean to say anything. Then when I found myself telling her, I was glad—I felt the whole matter was out of my hands."

Angus nodded. "And what did she suggest?"

"She agreed with me that Uncle Luke might know it was not a genuine *famille noire.* She told Johnnie."

The fingers stopped flicking pages. Angus looked at her.

"Yes?"

"I—I don't think that Johnnie will do anything about it either. You see, the lock isn't forced and Uncle Luke keeps the key on his key ring. So I have a feeling Johnnie thinks it's unlikely that there ever was an original."

Angus took out his cigarette case.

"Smoke?"

She wanted a cigarette badly. She wanted something to give her confidence for what she had come to say to Angus.

"I guess, we just leave the matter of the vase then. If two of the family know, it's for them to make the decision." He looked across the room at the lovely colors of the Paris copy, glowing against the black background.

Tess said, without looking at him, "Angus,

where can I sell some pieces of jewelry? They aren't terribly valuable, but some are antiques—"

"Don't you like them any more?"

"I love every one of them."

"Then why sell then?"

Whatever he was, whoever he was, Tess was certain that Angus would respect a confidence—she said, almost defiantly, "I'm not happy here. Oh, it's not the fault of Canada or—or anything to do with the country. It's a very personal thing, but I can't stay! I want to go back to England."

"Don't you think you should tell Johnnie, not me?"

"That's the one thing I can't do! If I *can* manage to go, it's got to be an—an escape—"

"Why do you put it like that?"

Tess walked to the window and looked out over the low shrubs, dazzling with snow as though overladen with blossom.

"I'm sorry, I—I can't tell you everything, Angus."

"No, I suppose you can't." He was silent for a moment then: "Tess, will you let *me* help you. I mean so that you don't have to sell your jewelry?"

"No—"

"Let me finish! I could advance you any

money you wanted and if you liked you could pay me back later—"

"I'm sorry, Angus. But I asked for your help *my* way, by telling me where I could go to sell some jewelry. Thank you for—for offering a much more practical way of helping, but *nothing* would make me accept! Please don't think I'm not grateful but—" She broke off, then turning from the window, cried, "I *can't*, Angus, I just *can't* accept that generous offer!"

"Very well, then, I'll find the name of a reliable jeweler for you—I don't know the Toronto shops that well myself—"

"Thank you!"

He sat on the edge of Luke's desk and regarded her with his brilliant, steady gaze.

"You haven't parents to go back to, Tess, have you? You told me they were dead. Have you relatives?"

"I have lots of good friends. Anyway, I can look after myself perfectly, once I get away from here."

Angus moved around the desk and stood in front of her. He said, gently:

"I think I'd do anything to help you get away, Tess—if only for a few months. I'd like to think of you now, *this very moment*, on a ship leaving for England! I'd like to think you'd come into this room to say good-bye!"

It was like a blow aimed at her secret love for him. An unconscious betrayal. She tried not to flinch, not even to let her gaze waver. He was ready to help her, always, in any way he could, but he didn't care if he never saw her again . . .

Suddenly he made a movement towards her; his hand felt for hers and drew her step by step towards him.

"You don't understand, Tess! How could you? I want you to go back to England, for a while at least, for your sake! I believe you will, because you have determination. Tess, go soon! I'll find a buyer for your jewelry today; go and sell it tomorrow—get away as quickly as you can! God help me, you're a married woman and I'm giving you this advice! But I can't help it because your peace of mind will always come first with me."

"Why *do* you want me to go? Angus, *why?*"

"I can't tell you that! Perhaps you'll never know. The onus is on me, Tess, and what I came here to do has ceased to be just an angry, calculating thing; it has become a terrible and doubtful responsibility."

"You're talking in riddles!"

"I'm sorry! It has to be that way because—" He broke off.

174

"Because—what?" her voice was a whisper.

"Personal feelings have crept in, Tess—mine for you! A man doesn't break up a marriage—but—"

She knew, then, knew that he loved her and that he would never actually say so.

"Angus—"

Nothing could stop that movement towards him, it was involuntary and almost unconscious.

His head was bent.

"I wish you were on that ship to England! Oh, Tess, Tess—if you knew how I wished it!" But his eyes and the grip of his hand and the whole vibrant aura around him said: *"I love you."*

There was a sound behind them. It seemed to Tess to come from a different world, and yet automatically their hands parted. They turned simultaneously towards the door.

Ginevra was entering. She said to Angus:

"You wanted some foolscap paper." Her eyes swiveled from one to the other. She smiled. She seemed to be mentally nodding her old head, knowingly, neither condoning nor condemning, standing apart, impartial as an ancient goddess.

"You're very cozy in here," was all she said. Then the door closed and they were alone again.

Angus drew a long breath.

Tess felt her body trembling so that she dare not try to cover up the moment by picking up her cup and drinking the now cold coffee.

"Sometimes," Angus said, "at some critical moment, fate steps in and shows you where your feet should be. On the ground, Tess, on the ground!" He smiled at her, took a book from the pile on the table and said: "When you came in I was just reading about the soothsayers of Japan—" He opened the book and showed her a colored photograph.

To Tess, looking at it, it was a jumble of pink and red and green—a meaningless picture she was pretending to be interested in. She knew that Angus was talking, telling her some story about Eastern soothsayers, covering up the silence. But for Tess the time had stopped when Ginevra opened the door. They had stood on the threshold before a moment that could have been beautiful and fatally foolish; a moment when they might have admitted their love. And, as though Ginevra had known by witchery, she had entered and slammed the magic door.

Tess heard herself say shakenly.

"If you've finished your coffee, Angus, I'll take your cup out with mine. I—I've got some work to finish for Uncle Luke."

"Of course—"

She dared to look at him and saw, to her infinite amazement, pain in his eyes. She turned quickly and went out of the room.

XII

FOR THREE DAYS Johnnie was his old self,
behaving with a lighthearted affection towards Tess. She did not, however, trust this
change in him. He was clever. Was he building
up a case against her so that she dare not
speak against him, whatever she might know?
It was subtle and insidious and Johnnie did
not overplay it. Just a warning, an emotional
scene to upset her, and then a period of calm
before the next climax. . . .

Tess could no longer bear Johnnie to touch
her. They lived in that house with an uneasy
truce between them and at night they slept as
though alone. Once, Johnnie tried to reach
out to her.

"Tess, don't let's go on like this."

She lay stiff and still, feeling his fingers
stroke her bare shoulder.

"Tess, darling, I shouldn't have been so
harsh with you, but then I was worried! Let's

178

start again—let's love one another. Tess—there's just a slit of moon shining in and I can see your face and your lovely shoulders."

Johnnie leaned towards her. Her wide open eyes saw the dark shadow of his face above her; felt his hands, tender on her body; saw his head bend as though he were about to kiss her. In a flash she pushed him aside and was out of bed. She seized her dressing-gown, felt in the darkness for her slippers and went to the door, feeling her way.

"Where are you going?"

"To the spare room."

"Oh no, you're not!"

He had swung himself off the bed and came after her. It was an eerie shadow-play. His arms reached out to catch her and she slipped from him. They could not see each other's faces, they were just slender moving shapes of blackness of the room with its one sliver of moonlight shining through the almost closed curtain on to her pillow.

Johnnie was stronger than Tess. He caught her before she could turn the handle of the door.

"Don't go! Tess, don't you realize that we can't let Uncle Luke think there's anything wrong between us? He sees us as a nice, happily married couple."

"Then he'll have to face the truth, won't he?"

There was a pause.

They stood quite still, their invisible faces turned towards one another.

"Don't be a little fool!" His voice seemed strange, coming not from him at all but from the room—like an echo. "If Uncle Luke has to know, Tess, then it will be *I* who will have his pity, not you. He has narrow, Calvinistic views, so *you* will be the one to be censured—"

Tess didn't move; her eyes ached with staring into the blackness.

"There comes a time, Johnnie, when threats no longer frighten! You hear them so often, you get a kind of protective armor against them. You can tell Uncle Luke anything you like about me only—*leave me alone!*" Despair gave her a sudden unexpected strength. She wrenched open the door, fled across the landing and into the spare room, closed the door as swiftly and silently as she could and locked it behind her.

Johnnie didn't come after her and she knew that he was afraid of waking the household. She stood for a moment in the new darkness and shivered. It was bitterly cold in here, because the room being unused, the radiator had not been turned on probably for weeks. She switched on the light and the room sprang into life. It was the kind of room to be seen in a home-making magazine: softly luxurious with its lovely green satin curtains sprigged with apple blossom; it's deep-piled pale pink rugs, its old walnut furniture. It was as gay and charming as a spring day. But for Tess it could have held an iron bedstead, a ragged curtain and a naked electric light bulb—she was beyond caring what the room looked like so long as she could be left in peace. . . .

Nobody the following morning mentioned the previous night's happenings. If anyone had heard a commotion, they ignored it. Johnnie behaved as though all was right with his world; his moods were unpredictable, yet his gaiety no longer rang true to Tess—it was like some charming cavalier costume he could put on at will.

On Thursday, the night Angus came to dinner, it snowed all day; huge flakes freezing as they touched the ground.

At breakfast Luke reminded Ginevra that Angus was coming that night.

"I haven't had a chance to see him and talk to him since he began on my books." He sat at the head of the table, his glass of orange juice standing in its bowl of cracked ice.

Behind the silver coffeepot, Ginevra's

hooded eyes lifted and met Tess' and became shuttered again.

"How long is this job going to take him?" she asked.

"Until I've seen him tonight how much he has done, I can't tell. It doesn't matter, anyway, so long as the work is done—"

Madrigal came in with a tray laden with eggs.

"M's Caswall says to tell you, suh!" She set down the dish of eggs on the side table.

"Well, girl, tell me what?" Luke's piercing eyes froze her.

"That, suh, there's an icicle agin, over the back door. It sur' is long, suh! I seen it."

"Ginevra"—Luke turned to his sister— "see to it today. It froze like the devil last night and the whole city will be chipping icicles from their porches."

Out of the window the falling snow made a thick white blanket over the avenue; even the trees lining the road were blocked out.

Luke turned to Johnnie. "You won't be able to go up to Chillawoka today."

"Not unless I want to commit suicide!" He grinned. "I'll ring the man I was taking up there and put him off. I've got someone who wants to go to Entobicoke. The road out there should be all right."

Olivia rose from the table. "By the way,

don't plan dinner for me, Aunt Ginevra. I'm going to the Club with the Cayleys."

"If they've got any sense," barked Luke, "they won't go."

"The Club is only up the road—" She pushed her chair in and went to the door. "Johnnie, would you be a dear and come and just look at the chains on my car?"

"Of course. Can you wait till I've had my breakfast?" His eyes were steady and smiling on her beautiful face. "You can do a morning's work on orange juice and toast, but *I* can't!"

"I'll be five minutes getting ready."

Luke said, "If it clears, I want to take Dalzell over to the Club tonight. There are a couple of books in the library there that I'd like him to see. He gets around and I want him to look out for copies for me. They were given to the Club by old Hull Macrankie back in the twenties. He'd roughed it all over China, and, boy, are those two books fascinating reading! I've had the booksellers here advertise for me, but they haven't had any replies. If Dalzell sees the Club copies, he'd be able to identify them if he saw them in a bookshop."

Angus didn't come that morning. He telephoned and left a message with Mary-Anne Caswall to say that he had some personal things he must do.

183

By evening the snow had stopped but it lay deep in the garden, loading down the branches of the trees.

Olivia had gone to dine at the club by the time Angus arrived. As always happened when he was there, Luke refused to talk about anything but the places he had once known. Angus did his best to include everyone in the conversation; Luke brought him back to Shanghai or Singapore. Angus asked Tess about the Royal Ballet in London where he had once seen Swan Lake and Ondine—Luke asked him if he'd seen the dancers of Bali.

After dinner, Luke had coffee sent to his study for himself and Angus. The rest went to the living-room. They heard the house staff leave, crunching through the snow.

Johnnie switched on the television. "I have some work to do on the Entobicoke lease. But there's a good program on tonight."

Ginevra said, "I'll be in to watch later. I've got some clearing up to do in the studio. Oh, and by the way"—she turned and faced them—"the bulb of my reading lamp went tonight and I didn't want to come all the way downstairs for another, so I went to take one from one of the spare room lamps. I found that someone is sleeping there."

"I am," Tess told her quietly. "But I didn't

tell you because—well—I didn't want to bother anyone. I mean—" she rushed on, "I'm keeping the room very tidy and making my bed—"

"That," Ginevra snapped, affronted, "is quite unnecessary. We have ample staff!"

"I know, Aunt Ginevra," Tess said quickly. "What I mean is—well—" She faltered.

"What Tess is trying to say," Johnnie put in, "is that it is only a very temporary arrangement and therefore nothing to make an issue over."

Ginevra looked from one to the other.

"Luke has little time for married couples who have separate rooms—"

"Oh, but we didn't at home and we don't intend to now, do we sweet?" His eyes sought Tess' but she refused to meet that bright, demanding gaze.

"There's no need at all for Uncle Luke to know," Johnnie went on as Tess didn't speak. "It really *is* only a temporary thing! Tess sleeps badly and she's a funny little thing, she doesn't want to disturb me and so she insists on a separate room until she gets over this insomnia bout."

Ginevra closed her eyes and sat quite quietly. Johnnie watched her.

"If you want the room, Aunt Ginevra—I

mean, if you have a guest coming to stay—"

She made a gesture with her hand.

"There are three guest rooms in the west wing for visitors. It's all right. I'll tell Madrigal to put a fresh bulb in the reading lamp and I think Hank had better see to the central heating radiator in there. It seems to have got an air-lock." She got up from her chair with difficulty—rheumatism gripped her when she sat for long—and crossed the room.

"Have you always slept badly, Tess?" she asked from the door.

"Oh no—I just—" She floundered again for words.

Ginevra cut in in her rasping voice: "Then I can't think why you do here. It's very quiet and you don't even hear the traffic along St. Clair. What disturbs you?"

"She has these nervy patches," Johnnie answered for Tess. "She's quite a highly-strung lady, this wife of mine! Not to worry."

"She hasn't struck me that way," Ginevra observed dryly.

"Anyway, she'll be back with me in a few days, won't you, sweet?" Johnnie's smile was bright; it touched his mouth so that he showed his fine white teeth, but it didn't touch his eyes. He followed Ginevra out of the room without a backward glance.

XIII

SHE SAT ALONE, watching, without much interest, the comedy-serial on television. Beyond the sounds in the room, she seemed to feel the quiet of the house.

An hour passed and Luke had not taken Angus to the Club. Then she heard the door of the study open.

"Ginevra? Tess?" he bellowed. "Where is everyone?" He came to the living-room door and flung it open. "There's a durned cat yowling outside my window. I tried to see if it's Ginevra's Faustus, but it's too dark and it wouldn't come when I called. I just looked in to see if it was here and the one outside was a stray."

"Shall I go and see for you, Uncle Luke?"

"You stay where you are. The wind's blowing straight from the Arctic tonight! I'll go." He slammed the door.

Tess turned off the television. A moment

later there was a crash and a loud, long-drawn shout of pain from somewhere in the house. There was a moment's deathly silence and then a burst of activity. Tess flew to the living-room door, rushed down the passage and heard a commotion at the back door.

She found the passage light on and the door open. Ginevra was there and Johnnie came racing down the back staircase.

Luke lay across the steps outside the door. He didn't move.

"What in heaven's name—" Johnnie cried.

Ginevra was on her knees by the old man. Swift realization of his danger made her drag off her coat and lay it over him even before she shouted to Johnnie to turn on the outside light.

The powerful bulb lit up the night. Angus came through the kitchen. "What's hap-pened—" At that moment he saw for himself and broke through the little group and bent down to the old man.

Swift, gentle, fingers felt the great inert body. Blood poured from a head wound.

"We must get him indoors. He mustn't lie out here in the freezing cold."

"But there may be broken bones—"

"There aren't—though it's a miracle in a man of his age and weight! Johnnie, take his feet. I'll take his head. It's more important to

188

get him indoors before we staunch the wound. Miss Bellairs, Tess—you'll have to help—he's a weight."

Luke seemed to rally for a moment or two, sufficiently to try to help himself but by the time they laid him on the couch in the sun-room he was unconscious again. Johnnie raced for blankets; Ginevra fetched water and bandages.

Luke was oblivious to it all. He lay on the settee with its orange and yellow cushions, blood staining the snow-white hair.

"This wound is dirty. Tess, get cotton wool," Angus said, "and ring up his doctor."

"But you could surely do what's necessary."

"Ring up, there's a good girl!" He didn't even turn to look at her.

Ginevra, however, was already at the telephone, calling the family doctor.

Tess flew to Angus with the cotton wool and towels.

"He's had a curious blow on the head—" Angus said, something sharp pierced him here, near the ear, as you see.

"He's a very heavy man to have fallen—"

"Very, but he fell easily—without tensing himself. Did you get on to his doctor?"

"Aunt Ginevra is doing that. But *he* can't do any more than you are doing—"

189

Angus said evasively, "Probably not, but he's *his* patient, not mine!"

"How *did* it happen, Angus?"

"I don't know. We'd been hearing a cat mewing somewhere and it was annoying your uncle. He had tried to see it through the window but couldn't; so he decided to come out and look for it."

Tess was aware of Ginevra and Johnnie entering the room.

"He's not like Faustus; he can't see in the dark and he never will turn those outside lights on!" Ginevra complained. "He must have caught his head against the step as he fell."

Tess saw a strange, closed look come down over Angus' face. Then the bell pealed and Johnnie went to the front door.

"That'll be his doctor," Ginevra said.

"Come along, Tess." Angus led her out of the room.

"As you're a doctor, don't you think you should stay?" she began.

But Angus had turned towards the back door. The outside light now blazed and the torch Ginevra had snatched up on her dash to see what had happened was lying on the small table just inside the door. Angus picked it up and walked to the outside steps and shone it down.

"I don't wonder he fell!" he said, "look at these chunks of ice."

Chunks of ice! Tess looked above her. A low balcony projected over the steps and the icicle which had hung there, the one Luke had told Ginevra to have removed, was no longer there. Small ones hung down, like little glistening points, but the great dangerous spear of ice had fallen shattering itself on the steps below.

"Do you think the icicle could have hit him?"

"It would have been a strange coincidence if it had fallen at the precise moment that he passed underneath it, wouldn't it, Tess?"

"Uncle Luke is a very big man; he's nearly six foot four. He might have knocked against it as he came out—"

Angus considered the balcony above him. "If it had been hanging that low, he'd have seen it as he walked into it—"

"He mightn't have done. It was very dark."

Johnnie came out, hunching himself in his coat.

"How did it happen, do you think?"

"That's what we're puzzling out."

"Did Aunt Ginevra tell Hank about it this morning?"

"I don't know." Johnnie looked at the ground. "Why, look at those chunks of ice!

That's *it!*" He kicked at a large chip. "But Hank wouldn't be such a loon as to leave the pieces there for someone to slip on!"

"The icicle would have made a clean wound, anyway," Angus said. "There was nothing clean about that gash on Mr. Bellairs' head." He flashed his torch.

Johnnie moved to Tess' side. "Madrigal mentioned the thing this morning at breakfast. I'll bet Aunt Ginevra forgot to tell Hank to break it up, and Hank never looks for work in winter. His mind hibernates until the spring!"

Then, small and clear and forlorn came the plaintive mewing of a cat.

"That's the sound we'd been hearing," Angus said. "It's around the side of the house, near the study."

"It must be Faustus, Aunt Ginevra's cat—" Johnnie said and moved forward. "He's such a pampered darling that an hour out in the snow would be his cat's idea of hell! I'll find him; he knows my voice; he'll come to me—"

"Odd that he stays there mewing when he hears our voices!"

"Yes, isn't it?" Johnnie said, and went around the side of the house.

Tess and Angus stood just inside the door, wrapped in their coats. *Strange,* Tess thought, *we're like people on the scene of a crime!* She checked her thoughts sharply. Only this was just an accident! Uncle Luke had fallen down the back steps and hurt his head. She stood by Angus' side, feeling at her back the warmth of the radiator in the small, back hall, and the cold of the luminous snow-world outside on her face.

"It's odd," she said, "about that cat—" And suddenly, on an impulse, she went out into the night and made her way around the house.

Johnnie was just by the study window, bending down, his hands busy with something.

Then she stared as the cat sprang out of the darkness and ears back, tail flying, shot past her into the house.

Johnnie came back.

"Silly thing! It was perched there, mewing its head off! Come Tess, you're shivering! I'll turn to ice myself if I stay out here much longer!"

Luke, more or less conscious, but inarticulate, was taken to his room. Johnnie saw the doctor out; Ginevra stayed to see that her brother was comfortable. She had insisted on a night nurse and one had been summoned by telephone. She came, and received her instructions from the doctor. The head wound had not been deep and complications were not expected. But the Bellairses were rich and could afford expensive nursing.

"His skull is like iron," Ginevra said. "And his tough early fighting days taught him how to fall. He'll be all right."

Olivia returned, shed her outdoor things and glanced at them with amusement.

"You look like a group of conspirators. What are you all plotting?"

Johnnie said, "There's been an accident," and told her about it.

"It *could* have been that icicle I forgot to tell Hank to break up," Ginevra said.

Olivia selected a cigarette from the box on the coffee table, let Angus light it for her, and looked at Johnnie.

"You mean that at the precise moment Uncle Luke was directly underneath it, it fell? Well, tell *that* to the Indians!" she derided.

"That's what I say—"

Tess watched the coal-black cat, sitting purring on Ginevra's lap. Why hadn't he come running when he heard them at the back door? And what had Johnnie been doing down by the study window?

She got up and went out of the room, picking up her coat from where she had dropped it on Aunt Stacey Bellairs' bridal chest in the hall.

194

Flinging it around her shoulders, Tess went out of the house by the back door.

Round by the study window there were thick clumps of bushes against the wall. Perhaps, she thought, the cat had got himself entangled. But cats don't! They could walk with velvet feet, unscathed, through any tangle. Tess bent down and saw, by the faint moonlight, that some of the branches were dark as though snow had been shaken off them by movement. And among them, right underneath the study window, she found an old sack. It felt clammy and sodden against her frozen hand.

Immediately she knew! Someone had put Ginevra's cat in that sack and set it there underneath the window, hidden in the bushes. There were holes in it so that the animal could breathe but it would have been difficult for it to extricate itself.

But everyone in the house loved Aunt Ginevra's plush, beautiful pet! No one would harm Faustus; but someone might have tied him in the sack in order to draw Uncle Luke into the garden to investigate.

"Yes," said a voice behind her, and she swung around to find Johnnie watching her. "Yes, Tess, it worked, didn't it? But not quite as well as was expected."

She dropped the sack she was holding and turned away. Johnnie picked it up.

"That's how I found him, tied up in this. He wasn't hurt." He pitched the sack into the hedge. "Come inside."

She walked without a word past him and into the house. In the kitchen, Johnnie said:

"Does it occur to you, Tess, that there are two people it could have been who did this?"

"You talk as though it was deliberate!"

"A cat doesn't tie itself up in a sack—so somebody wanted to draw Uncle Luke outside."

"But who?"

"Ginevra—or you—"

Tess didn't even flinch.

"Why are you leaving out Olivia?"

"She only came in after it had happened—"

"Since your thoughts are working in that direction, Johnnie, playing around with suspects, let's include Olivia. She could have been here earlier, couldn't she? And then again, what about *you?*"

He laughed in her face.

"That's not very bright of you! I was upstairs in my study. The very moment I heard the commotion I came rushing down the stairs. Aunt Ginevra was already there and she saw me come down. Unless, of course, you think I harmed Uncle Luke by remote control!"

It was a cast-iron alibi and she realized it.

"Of course," Johnnie was saying, "we're forgetting Angus."

"Why on earth should a perfect stranger want to harm Uncle Luke? It was Angus, anyway, who said that the wound was too dirty to have been caused by the icicle and that if he'd hit his head against the step, the wound wouldn't have been so sharp."

"It could have been policy to say that, since we were all there and it would probably have occurred to one of us. It's an old dodge, Tess, to be the first to point out the facts that others are bound to see sooner or later!"

"Just because Angus came as a stranger—you—dare to suspect him!" Fear as well as anger heightened her voice.

"But Tess, you see for yourself that odd things are happening in this house since you—and Angus—came! We lived a calm, comfortable existence till then—we really played at 'happy families'!"

"I didn't manufacture those footsteps I heard when I arrived!" she cried.

He didn't seem to hear her.

"Then there's the matter of the *famille noire* vase. Since you listened in to that recorded conversation, you know that Olivia told me."

"Yes."

"I think," Johnnie said, "when Uncle Luke is better, I'll have to take a risk on his hoaxing us about it, and tell him we know it's only a copy. I decided at the time I heard about it, to let it be—because Uncle Luke may be reckoning on no one he shows it off to knowing the difference between a K'ang Hsi and the Paris copies. You see I've been thinking about the things that have been happening, and I've got a theory—" He waited. "Aren't you going to ask me what it is?"

"No!" She leaned against the table. "You intend to tell me, anyway—"

"Yes, sweet, I do! Suppose when Angus first saw the vase he remembered where he had seen a copy? Suppose he bought it—and it's my guess it cost him a pretty penny! Well, keys can be duplicated if you know how—*I* don't, and for all his money, Uncle Luke is too darned mean to have special locks or safety devices anywhere! Angus is in the study a lot so he had plenty of time—"

"And I suppose he carried the vase through the house in daylight," she cried in angry derision. "Wrapped in a copy of the *New York Times*!"

"There are ways. He could have brought the copy by night and hidden it somewhere—

say in the peony bushes outside Uncle Luke's study window. He had only to open the window while he was shut up in the study, exchange the vases and then come back sometime when it was dark and pick up the genuine one."

"You make up a good story, Johnnie." She heard her hard scathing voice, violently and desperately refusing to acknowledge its feasibility.

"And then tonight, perhaps Uncle Luke got a little bit suspicious of him. Suppose he has missed one or two of his most valuable books?"

"And I suppose Angus carried *those* out under his arm in broad daylight. Or does he have a poacher's pocket?"

But Johnnie didn't heed her bitter derision; he was absorbed in his theory.

"And so, he might have tried to kill Uncle Luke."

"Hoping that the million-to-one chance would happen and an icicle would fall just at the right moment? How twisted can your mind get?" she blazed at him.

"Come to that, why are you such a champion of a man you'd like us to think you scarcely know?"

She pushed past him without answering,

knowing that the color had rushed to her face. High heels tapping, she walked into the living-room and saw that Angus had risen and was on the point of leaving.

He smiled at her, and it was one bleak moment of warmth in all that doubt and mystery. Ginevra's cat, curled up on her lap, looked at Tess with green fire in his eyes.

If he could speak, she thought, he'd tell who had done this thing. But it wasn't Angus—it mustn't have been Angus. . . .

XIV

HAD SOMEONE TRIED to harm Uncle Luke tonight? As everyone had said, it was too much coincidence that the icicle had fallen at the very moment he had walked beneath it; and although the lumps of ice on the step could have resulted in his fall, it would not have caused that single sharp blow dangerously near the fatal spot by the ear. . . .

"You're shivering, Tess," Olivia's voice startled her.

"I—I suppose I got cold out there by the back door!"

You've got the loudest purr I know!" Angus broke in, addressing the cat, turning the conversation. "It's like a drumbeat. You should be called Drum-Major!"

Good night's were said and Johnnie said he would see Angus out. The living-room door was pulled to behind them.

"Good night, Dr. Dalzell!" Olivia said softly, when they had gone. "Only he isn't a doctor, is he, Tess? Did *you* know that, Aunt Ginevra?"

"What do you mean?" She sat up so briskly that the cat jumped, offended from her lap.

"There's no such name as Angus Dalzell in the Vancouver medical list. Tess knows it, too!"

Ginevra sat, hands lying along the arms of her chair.

"So! Then who is he? And why does he call himself 'Doctor'?"

Olivia rose with a swing of a red silk skirt.

"Oh, it lends respectability to one, doesn't it? And Canada is a huge place—who'd query it? Who—except a suspicious, nasty person like me?" Her smile was brilliant. "Do we tell Uncle Luke?"

"If what you say is true, then we certainly do!"

Olivia nodded. "It's true, all right! Tess can vouch for that."

"Why didn't you tell me this before?" Ginevra looked at them from under her heavy lids.

"Oh, I've only just found out. Ask Tess why she didn't tell you. She's probably known all along."

"Angus is a friend of some friends of mine.

They like him and trust him—"

"And so," snapped Ginevra, "if he'd called himself the Count of Monte Cristo, you'd have let it pass! You had no right to keep this knowledge to yourself! You should have told me, at least."

"I'm sorry, Aunt Ginevra, but you know now—as much as I do. There's nothing— *nothing* more I can tell you. If you don't mind I'd like to go to bed now." She didn't wait for Ginevra to ask more questions; she wouldn't have been able to answer them, anyway. She had spoken the truth when she had said. "I know nothing—*nothing!*"

Angus had gone and the hall was empty. Tess went up to the spare room and switched on the light. Johnnie had been waiting in the dark for her.

"I just came to draw the curtains and see that the heating is working. The radiator in this room is always getting air-locks."

"Please leave me alone."

"Get into bed. Don't sit up reading—"

"I may, for a while."

"Not tonight! Just get into bed. I'm going to tuck you up and bring you some hot milk."

"I don't want any."

He said, "It's been an exhausting evening. It'll help you to sleep."

It was no use arguing, but directly he had gone she flew to the door to lock it. The key had gone. One of the other door keys would probably fit, she thought, and went along the corridor, looking. There were no keys in the doors. But there *had* been until tonight. . . .

Tess gave in. She went back, undressed and got into bed and lay quite still, staring up at the fine, molded ceiling.

Johnnie returned with a tray. On it was a glass of milk and by its side a blue capsule.

"Look, sweet, take this. It's quite harmless and it'll give you a lovely, dreamless sleep."

Just some hot milk? She didn't know. She, wouldn't know until she had drunk it—and then perhaps she would never know! Perhaps there was more sedative in the milk—too much . . . *too much* . . . and they'd say: *"That's the way it is! She couldn't bear to think of what she'd done and what she might do in the future . . . an overdose—"*

Johnnie was sitting on the edge of the bed watching her.

"Drink it up, Tess. It'll do you good. And don't worry, I'll look after you—"

She reached for the glass. The soft hypnotism of Johnnie's eyes forced her to pick up the tablet, swallow it and drink the milk.

"Now let me alone."

"Of course, sweet! Good night."

She turned her face away before he could kiss her, and lay still, waiting. But he went to the window and pulled aside the curtain and looked out. With his back to her, he said:

"Tess, tell me one thing before I go. You *do* remember every moment of tonight, don't you?"

"Of course! Why—?"

"Sweet, you must forgive me, but I've got to ask it. You haven't been dwelling on what I said—about never letting you go while Uncle Luke is alive? You didn't—without fully realizing what you were doing, take—well—take the matter into your own hands tonight? You didn't let your mind dwell on the possibility of being free if anything happened to Uncle Luke—dwell too much on it, so that—oh Tess—" He swung around and regarded her.

Tess couldn't have moved, had she wanted to. She felt turned to stone by this last suggested horror! What he was really asking, was "Could you *have attacked Luke* subconsciously?" Useless to tell herself that the whole thing was ludicrous. This house was like a stake to which she was tied and tongues of evil flame were hissing about her.

She managed to speak, to say with a flash of spirit:

"What you are meaning is that you *want* to believe I tried to harm Uncle Luke—"

He was by her bedside.

"Tess, don't you see, I'm trying to think out what could have happened? I've *got* to talk it over with someone—to discuss every possibility—"

She closed her eyes against the hypocritical anxiety in his. He must be glad she had come to bed so that he could get the family alone and talk it out and perhaps turn their minds to the conclusion that Tess had done this thing; Tess, whose coming to the house had precipitated so many strange happenings. . . .

"When Uncle Luke is better," she said in a firm voice, "I'm going to him and I am going to tell him about the car accident. I'm going to tell him exactly what the doctor said, that it was shock and there was no likelihood of its recurrence. I shall tell him, too, how frightened you are that I may still be ill."

"If you feel it would help, by all means do that, Tess. Yes, *do* that!" he said with a surprising urgency in his voice. "But, for the moment, just go to sleep and don't worry about anything."

When he had gone out of the room, she lay wondering why he had encouraged her in the idea to tell Uncle Luke. And suddenly she knew. Of course he would speak first. He, the charming nephew—a kinsman—normal and uncomplicated would tell Uncle Luke about it before she had the chance, putting his own interpretation on it all. Perhaps he was going downstairs now to prepare the way. . . . Olivia would be his ally. And Ginevra?

What were they saying? Her wits, which had been dulled by the shock of the happenings of that evening, seemed suddenly to take on a sharpness; a last desperate spree of clear thought, perhaps, before the drug took control of her mind.

The drug! How much? *How much had she been given in the milk itself?*

Tess struggled to her feet; slipped her feet into slippers, put on her blue housecoat and felt it cool against warm flesh. Then she went downstairs.

There was a light in the hall and she heard the night nurse moving about in Uncle Luke's room. Not a single stair of the elegant, curved staircase creaked as she made her way down to the hall. She went past the living-room, down the passage and through the kitchen to the sunroom. A door there opened into the living-room. She knew that it was hidden on the other side by rose brocade curtains and a small table on which stood a golden Buddha.

Tess paused, her fingers around the handle of the door and listened to the murmur of conversation. When a moment came in which all three seemed to be talking at once, she opened the door a few inches hoping that the noise of their voices would drown any sound the handle might make.

". . . so Uncle Luke came to while you were with him, Aunt Ginevra?"

"For a moment, yes."

"And he didn't say what hit him?"

"No. He just murmured 'Blow. Blow.' Twice. And then he was unconscious again."

Johnnie said, "Wait! Let me think. If it was deliberate, who could want to do such a thing?"

"There's always Uncle Luke's phony doctor—" Olivia said. "Tess brought him here—"

"Yes, I know. And there's something I want to say to you, now that we're together—something about Tess," Johnnie began. "I think you know that before I married her she was involved in an accident that killed both her parents. What you don't know is that she had a breakdown, through shock, and suffered blackouts. I've been wondering—"

"Wondering what, Johnnie?" Olivia asked softly.

"Well, she's behaving a little oddly!"

"Go on!"

"I can't!" he cried. "She's my wife, after all. Oh hell! What does a man do?"

"Tell us what's on your mind, Johnnie dear," Olivia said, still softly. "We're family, you know, we stick together."

"I don't know what to say! When I went upstairs just now, Tess was in a very agitated state. I left her to drink her milk but I wondered whether I ought to call you, Aunt Ginevra. She wants sleeping tablets, but I—"

There was more, much more, but Tess didn't hear it. Suddenly everything seemed to be swinging about her—the curtain, the wall, as though they had sprung alive. Tess swayed, too. And then crashed against the door. She heard the little table on the other side fall; she heard the thud of the heavy gilded Buddha. Dimly she was aware of people, of faces—sharp, startled, suspicious. . . .

This is what Johnnie wanted to happen. . . .

She tried to make one gigantic effort to speak and she thought she did say something, just one word that sounded like a name—the very last name she wanted to say. *Angus!* For the love of heaven she had only, surely, said it in her mind! *Angus!* It was as though she had no power to stop herself! And then another thought dazzled terrifyingly through the on-coming numbness. *One capsule wouldn't do this, wouldn't knock me out—so—completely! Then there was more—in the drink! How much—how much—?* And then everything be-came a blank.

XV

TESS WAS AWARE of light playing on her eyelids. She blinked and looked about her. Through the soft pink nylon curtains sunbeams danced on the charming gaiety of the room. She lay for a moment or two, gathering her thoughts, pulling herself out of the heavy sleep into a wakefulness that could recall all that happened.

By her side, on the polished bedside table, was the little hand-painted tray with the empty glass that had contained her milk. As though it were the switch that illuminated all her mind, memories rushed in. She had drunk that milk with some wild, extravagant fear that there could have been an overdose of sedative in it. She had got up and gone downstairs, partly to know what Johnnie might say of her and partly in some desperate desire for self-preservation, to be near help should she

211

collapse. And there *had* been a sedative in the milk—the single capsule on the tray could not have had such a drastic effect as to knock her out so completely. But her imagination had taken her too far. Of course Johnnie would not give her a lethal dose!

Someone had carried her to bed and someone had entered the room this morning and drawn the curtains to wake her. She saw that her aquamarine silk housecoat had been neatly folded across a chair, her bunny scuffs were by her bed. Set together as neat and prim as though a little Victorian child wore them.

The door opened and Johnnie came in, carrying a tray.

"So you're awake. It's nine o'clock and I thought I'd bring up your breakfast."

Every bedroom in the house had its small colored bed-table. He set it up, placed her breakfast before her and said:

"Coffee, toast and orange juice, your usual frugal meal, sweet!"

She thought that he looked strained, but that could have been a trick of light.

"It's a lovely morning but there are strict instructions from Aunt Ginevra that you're to lie in till late."

"I don't need to. I'm perfectly all right. How is Uncle Luke?"

"Quite literally like a bear with a sore head! A man with a thinner skull might have been killed. As it is, he's propped up on his pillows, perfectly conscious. He has sent the nurse away and is demanding that Aunt Ginevra ring that 'Goddarned doctor,' and let him get up." He smiled at her. "Now, enjoy your breakfast. Do you want some music?" He indicated the switch that each bedroom had, connecting with the master radio in the kitchen. Mary-Anne worked to music.

"I passed out last night, didn't I?"

He said evenly, "You did, and I carried you up to bed. What in the world did you come down for, Tess? Did you leave your library book in the sunroom? But you should have rung for someone to fetch it for you."

Tess let the suggestion pass. She thanked him for the breakfast and said, I don't want any music, Johnnie." *(Go! Go!* she willed silently.)

But she knew as he paused at the door and looked across at her, that he knew perfectly well she had not gone into the sun-room for a book. His manner told her quite clearly that he had not finished with that incident yet and that sooner or later there would be more questions, more insinuations.

When the door had closed behind him, she

poured out coffee, lit a cigarette and lay back. Had it been an accident last night, or had someone made an attack, which had failed, on Uncle Luke's life? And if so, who? Johnnie had been upstairs; Olivia had been out; Ginevra had a kind of wry affection for her brother. Tess remembered with dismay Johnnie's hints about Angus, and rejected them.

Then *who?* And why? She saw with horror how easy it would be for people to suspect her!

"While Uncle Luke is alive, I shall never let you go!" Johnnie had said. And on that he would base his suspicion of her; would hint and plant doubts about her in the minds of the rest of the family. Because, in the end, he would get free of *her!* A whole fortune was better than half, as Olivia had put it. "The whole lovely lot . . . Johnnie darling!" Well, Tess thought, lying there in the winter sunlight, she would make it easy for him; she would go back to England. She would say: "I can't be away from my home too long. One of us must be there." And if Luke said, "Go back and sell up and come and live here," then she would quietly acquiesce, leave them all as inconsequently as though she were coming back—and then write from England and tell Johnnie she could never live with him again. One thing she must not do, and that was to let

214

anyone know that she had no intention of returning. She must precipitate no scene.

So, she would return to England, begging, borrowing or stealing the money. She thought of her small pieces of jewelry—she must remind Angus that he had promised to let her know where she could best sell them!

Then there was her watch and camera. She knew she dare not go for help to the British authorities out here because they would do nothing without first getting in touch with Johnnie.

Tess was up and nearly dressed when he came in.

"I told Madrigal not to disturb you in case you'd gone off to sleep again. You were told"—he gave her a gently punishing look— "to stay in bed for most of the morning."

"Uncle Luke is the invalid, not I."

Johnnie didn't take the tray and go. Instead he sat himself down on the dressing-table stool and watched her.

"You'll be late for whatever work you have to do," she began.

"I want to hang around a bit; the doctor's coming this morning."

"Does Uncle Luke know—what—hit him?"

Johnnie gave her a strange look.

"He thinks the top of his head caught that

icicle. He's mad at Ginevra for forgetting to tell Hank to break it up."

"Perhaps he really did catch his head against it." Tess slid her arms into the red sweater and pulled it over her head. Then she reached over Johnnie to get her comb.

He caught her wrist.

"Tess, I've got to talk to you! I've had a sleepless night over all this."

"It won't do any good talking to *me*."

"There are only three possible explanations for what happened last night."

"You've probably discussed it fully with the family," she said coldly. "I don't want to hear."

"But you heard quite a bit last night, didn't you? You're making a habit of listening at keyholes, aren't you?"

She stiffened, tensing her body away from him. "Will you move, please, Johnnie? I want to get my shoes out of the closet."

He didn't stir. His eyes watched her every movement.

"What did you expect to hear through that door?"

"What I had every right to!" she said quietly. "If I'm your wife, I'm part of the family—I'm not supposed to be put to bed and given a sedative in order to be kept out of the way!"

"Aunt Ginevra is certain that what happened is no accident! She's determined to tell Uncle Luke so when he's better! As I said, there are three possibilities, Tess, the first is Dalzell. Of the other two, Aunt Ginevra refuses to believe that Uncle Luke really hit that icicle."

"He'd have seen it, anyway!"

"Except that, of course, without the outside light on—and trust Uncle to go bull-rushing about in the dark!—he mightn't have seen it. But I agree with Aunt Ginevra. You don't walk into a spear of ice! So—"

She said with cool patience, "Johnnie, may I *please* get my shoes?"

Before she could avoid him, he rose and his arms went around her. "Oh Tess, Tess!" His voice was low, urgent. "Darling, try to understand that whatever happens, I'll stand by you! Some people *do* do things they can't help, things they don't even remember doing—"

She fought in his arms.

"You must listen—"

The only way to release that iron grip was to scream. And Uncle Luke's room was too near her to dare to do that! The alternative was rigid resistance, to make herself like a stone in Johnnie's arms. She looked down, refusing to meet his eyes.

"Tess, I've been thinking, puzzling all night.

Say you didn't try to harm Uncle Luke—*say it,* darling! You see, it must have been one of two people—Angus—or you! And then I remembered how you had spoken about that icicle over the front porch when you first came and that perhaps the idea—"

"I had *no* idea," she said in a desperately controlled voice. "After Madrigal mentioned it at breakfast I never thought about it again!"

"Then don't you see? That leaves Dalzell!"

Either herself—or the man she loved! The trap was neatly laid to ensnare one or other—or both—almost as though it were deliberate; as though someone knew that she loved Angus! But that was impossible! Impossible, in this house of watching eyes?

Johnnie had dropped his arms from her and turned to the window. His hands went to his head; he thrust his fingers through his hair—that fine, bright corn-colored hair that made him seem so boyish, so disarming.

"Tess, I hate to harp on this, but I've got to! You admit that you asked the doctor what you had done during those lost hours. You told me so."

"I also told you that the doctor laughed at me—that it was a purely temporary thing. It couldn't possibly come back!"

Johnnie's silence was eloquent. It said: *Doc-*

218

tors have been known to be wrong.

Tess heard a sound outside the room. She called loudly:

"Madrigal!"

The door opened and the maid put her pretty head around, blinking shyly at them.

"Would you take that tray downstairs, please?" Tess asked.

She seized her shoes from the closet, put them on and before Madrigal could pick up the tray, she was out of the room.

Ginevra was in the hall. She had on her beautiful ranch mink coat and a black headscarf. She was standing by the radiator under one of the tall windows.

"I've just been around this house with Hank," she said, "looking for killer icicles because that's what my brother seems to think hit him."

"But didn't Angus say last night that an icicle is a relatively clean thing and the wound was dirty?"

Ginevra didn't answer Tess' question, but her eyes regarded her thoughtfully.

"Aunt Ginevra, it was an accident, wasn't it?"

"You can think so. I don't. Strange things are happening here," said the old woman. "Things that have got to be stopped. When Luke is better, I'm going to have a talk with him. Until then, I think it's best if we don't discuss it."

Because one of the things to be discussed is me! Tess thought. *Because last night Johnnie dropped incriminating hints about me!*

The day was a strange one. The house had an air of waiting, like a polite listener to a conversation only half finished. Johnnie went in to see his uncle and then left for the office. Tess went out too, announcing that she would not be in for lunch. She spent two hours in the library and then lunched at one of the downtown stores. In the afternoon she took a bus along the lakeside drive. Lake Ontario stretched around her, a vast inland sea, glittering in the fitful winter light. In the distance she saw the island which in summer, Johnnie told her, was crowded with yachtsmen and sunbathers.

She was tired and cold when she arrived home to find Ginevra out and Mary-Anne Caswall and Madrigal in charge of Luke. She went to see him and found him dozing over a pile of papers, the bandage tilted a little over one eye, like a rakish crown. He was pleased to see her, but cross that he was being kept inactive. However, he seemed to think that was no reason why others shouldn't be kept occupied, and gave her some lists of figures and a report to type for him.

Tess went from his room to the bedroom she had refused to share any longer with Johnnie. There she opened her small jewel case and made a little heap of the things she planned to sell. She laid aside a Victorian garnet necklace and the pearl and turquoise ring that had belonged to her grandmother. For a moment she played with them, moving them backwards and forwards on the glass surface of the dressing-table, remembering with nostalgia her charming grandmother, only four feet, eleven inches in height but holding herself up to the day of her death like a little queen. Then she took out her mother's diamond solitaire and the garnet bracelet she remembered her father had given her on her birthday. Two gold bangles and a cultured pearl necklace she had bought herself with some money her grandmother had left her. There they were, a little pile of treasures, so beloved that it hurt to part with them. But this was not a moment for sentiment; she was desperate to get away, to feel the freedom of a life where there was no suspicion, no subtle insinuations, no destructive enmity.

She wrapped each piece in cotton wool and put them into a red and white sponge bag which had been a gift from a colleague in London.

Then she took the papers Luke had given her and went into the small sitting-room and began to type.

She heard Ginevra come in and go upstairs to her brother's bedroom. At some time after five, Olivia returned from work and then Johnnie's car came up the drive.

Dinner that evening was not a comfortable meal. The happenings of the previous night lay heavily between them, touched upon and shied away from; to be spoken of, perhaps, among themselves but never in front of Tess.

XVI

TESS WAS CERTAIN that Angus would call the following day, if not to work, then to inquire about Luke. But he neither came nor telephoned. She found herself waiting and watching for him, fighting back the fear in her mind that he wouldn't come at all—that, in fact, he would never come again.

If that were so, then she knew how deeply and terribly her lurking suspicions would rise up and taunt her. The strange train of events since she had arrived could start working backwards, each one cementing the doubts all the Bellairs family, save Luke, held about Angus.

Did old Luke become suspicious last night about Angus? Did he link him with the strange happenings in the house? Had Angus been prowling around the house the other night and had he dropped the note in the letter box purely to safeguard himself should anyone see him?

From there, back to the mystery of the K'ang Hsi vase.

Back farther to the first meeting between Luke and Angus. Had he known that the old man had a passion for travel and had he played on that to get an introduction to the house? If so, the gods were most certainly with him that Luke was wanting someone to arrange and catalogue his book! Had Angus had previous knowledge of the old man through some mutual friend?

She had pushed these thoughts away so many times. But at last, standing by the window of the spare-room which was her temporary bedroom, they finally struck and would not leave her.

She clapped her hands to her ears as though her thoughts came from outside herself, swarming in upon her like the small devils that leapt at Pandora when the magic box was opened.

Angus is not a criminal. I'd know if he was— something would warn me; some small thing communicate itself to me and give me a clue. I couldn't love him if he were evil. . . . I couldn't trust him if he were a liar. But the argument sprang back at her, mocking her. She had loved Johnnie and he had evil in him; and now she loved a man whom the world would condemn as an imposter.

Alarm, anxiety, desperation welled up in her with such force that what she did next was from a compulsion far stronger than herself.

She dragged on her coat and hat; ran down the stairs oblivious of who should hear or see her frantic state, and got her overshoes from the cloakroom in the hall.

No one was around. She flung open the street door and slammed it behind her.

She was going to Angus; going to see him and make him tell her why he had lied, saying that he was a doctor, saying that he came from Vancouver. . . . He was going to tell her the truth about himself and she would refuse to leave until he did.

The side street was slippery with the frozen remains of swept snow; but Tess was getting used to maneuvering her steps so that she didn't slip and slide. When she reached St. Clair Avenue, walking was easier.

Angus lived in a hotel only two blocks away. She walked quickly down the beautiful street, only vaguely aware of the traffic, the towering buildings, the high, saffron-tinted clouds hanging around the northern skyline, presaging more snow.

The hotel where Angus was staying was a

fine, smallish modern building, neither garish nor façaded in ornamental stone. It stood solid and quiet behind the line of bare trees and Tess walked up the steps and straight to the "Inquiry" desk without letting herself stop to think. She didn't dare, or her courage would fail her.

"Dr. Dalzell?"

Immediately she asked for him she had a dreadful feeling that they would tell her he had gone and left no forwarding address. Instead, when she gave her name, the clerk contacted his room. There was no reply.

"Would you like us to page him?"

She shook her head. "No, I—I'll just look around the lounge," she said quietly, "and if he isn't there, I'll leave a note for you to give him."

She walked towards the lounge, glancing in at the writing room as she went.

There were a number of people in the circular lounge with tall green plants trailing up a trellis on one wall, and the muted clatter of coffee cups and conversation met her at the open glass doors.

It would be hopeless finding him in this crowd, she thought, unless she made a slow inspection of the room, and she was too aware of eyes turned towards her, to do this. She should be inconspicuous for such a task and glancing aside at herself in a mirror, she realized that she was wearing her tomato red coat—the one nearest at hand—and a sky-blue beret. She was about as conspicuous as a gigantic flower in a snow field—her thoughts faded and her heart turned over. There was Angus seated at a corner table with a girl in a silver muskrat coat, her dark curly head bare. Angus had seen her and was saying something to the girl that made her turn and look at Tess. For a frozen moment she stood there, unable to escape. Angus was explaining something to the girl, who was frowning and then shaking her head as though in bewildered protest.

The next moment they had both risen and Angus was striding towards Tess. Quickly, moved by impulse, she turned and fled. But, aware that he would catch her up if she made for the door, she darted into the small, deserted writing room hoping that he had lost her in the groups standing around the lobby and that he would go by and look for her in the street.

"Tess!"

He stood before her, blocking her escape.

Helplessly she looked up at him.

"What in heaven's name are you doing here?" His tone was almost violent.

"I—I wanted to see you—"

"What's happened?"

"Plenty!" she said with returning courage. "You should know that, since you were at the house the other night!"

"How is your uncle?"

"You could have called and inquired!" Nerves made her fly to the attack.

"My dear Tess, I knew perfectly well that he'd be all right. It was a superficial wound and his heart was in fine condition. The—accident wouldn't kill him!"

"Nevertheless, as a friend of the family, you could have rung up to find out!"

He looked down at her, his expression enigmatic.

"Good manners should have made me inquire—I know that, Tess. But there were more important considerations. It was better that I—" He broke off, looking up and away from her.

"That you, what?" she prompted.

"That I put all thoughts of the Bellairs house out of my mind!" His voice was rough.

A despair swept her. She saw that for reasons of his own, he wanted no more contact with any of them and that she would lose even his strange friendship. She would, from now on, be more terribly alone than ever.

She pulled herself together. At least in front of this man who never wanted to see her again, she would appear calm.

"That's all right, Angus," she said, almost loftily. "After all you're—you're a stranger to us; you're perfectly free not to want to see any of us again, but—"

"But what?"

"I think you might have told me," she said in a small voice.

His laugh was sharp and had an edge of bitterness.

"You've no idea how ironical that is, Tess! It was so good knowing you that I wanted to say good-bye to you least of all—"

She looked down at the floor, saying overbrightly:

"That's that, then! There was a song, my father had a gramophone record of it. It went: 'Thanks for the memory.' Well—thanks, then!"

"Stop it, Tess!" He reached out as though to touch her, and then his arm dropped to his side.

She heard him catch back words.

"Hadn't you better go back to—to—whoever you were having coffee with?" she suggested.

"That was Lena Crane—she was at the University with me and we met here unexpectedly. She's gone, anyway. She had an appointment at the Medical Center here."

"Or did you send her away so that you could come and see what I wanted?"

"Right, I did! I said: 'Scram, honey, there's a girl over there who I believe has come to look for me and I'd better see what she wants'—and do you know what she said?"

"Am I interested?"

"Of course. We all want to know what other people say of us. She said: 'Your young friend looks as though she'd been living with ghosts.' "

"I doubt it—if that's complimentary enough to have been repeated—" She spoke rigidly, trying to pass him. But he was in her way.

"She said it kindly because you stood there, Tess, with a kind of lost aura around you—and you're very pale. You don't go out enough in this lovely crisp air. Have you been out walking in the country since you and I went to the Farraway?"

She shook her head.

"Why not?"

"Because—well, because Johnnie hates walking anyway and—" She broke off as someone entered the room, pushing past Angus.

He said impatiently: "We can't talk here. Come out to the car; it's parked just around the back."

230

She had said nothing yet that she had wanted to say to him, and she went willingly enough.

He settled her in her seat, offered her a cigarette, took one himself and lit them both. Then he started the car, turning into University Avenue and out, away from the town.

They drove in silence for some minutes; then he asked:

"What did you want to see me about?"

She couldn't ask all the things she wanted to while he drove along the crowded roads; better wait until they had reached a quieter spot so that, if he were angry with her, he wouldn't vent it on the steering-wheel and jeopardize their lives! At once she pulled her thoughts up. This was crazy, thinking in terms of melodrama all the time, she who used to take life so lightly, so joyfully! But things were working that way recently, and she was caught up in a maelstrom that could end in tragedy . . . *had* nearly ended that way two nights ago.

She started as Angus laid a hand lightly on her arm.

"I'm sorry I was short with you back there in the hotel, but it was a shock seeing you. I had made up my mind that I would never set foot in that house again, and somehow I didn't expect to see you at the hotel."

"Why weren't you coming to the house again?"

He stepped on the accelerator.

"You should know—"

"How can I?"

He turned off, without answering, into a narrow road running between fields. In the distance new houses were being built but here, along this rough road, there was nothing but the stretches of rich earth lying under the great blanket of snow and trees, unmoving in the windless morning.

Angus stopped the car and switched off the engine. Then he threw his cigarette out of the window, turned to her and answered her question.

"I am in love with you."

She sat quite still, and through her fear of all that he might be, came the singing joy again. She felt him reach for her left hand, looking down at her two rings.

"This," he said, and his finger touched them, "is the reason I decided never to see any of you again."

She felt herself trembling and he took his hand away.

Staring ahead of her, seeing nothing but a blur of white, she said, "I love you, too, Angus."

"That makes it even more complicated!" His tone was matter-of-fact.

"But you know! You must have—"

"I told myself it was wishful thinking."

She sat quite still, hearing herself ask: "What are we going to do, Angus?"

"For God's sake, Tess, if you had any idea of the responsibility I bear—of the hours I've given to thought, to wondering what I *should* do—for all our sakes—"

"Johnnie doesn't love me."

He seemed not to hear and went on: "I was going to slip out of your lives; I was going to shelve all my plans, all that I had come here to do!"

"What had you to do? You're talking in riddles."

"I know—I have to. I daren't tell you the truth, Tess."

"About—yourself?"

"About so much!" He turned to her and suddenly she was in his arms, and his mouth was on hers. One hand took her beret from her head and then she felt his fingers in her hair, felt his palm cup her head, drawing her closer to him.

A car, hooting at something on the highway, startled the silence. He drew away from her, picked up her blue beret from where it had fallen on the floor of the car, and lit another cigarette.

The brief interlude of averred mutual love, the pulsating fervor of kisses was over. He was so matter-of-fact again that she might have dreamed those moments or seconds or minutes—she had no idea how long she had been in his arms. When the spirit reaches the stars, time has no meaning.

Angus stirred, blew a coil of smoke and said, "I'm in a quandary, Tess, and telling you won't help. In fact I can't—I daren't tell you! So, we'd better go back. It's not safe being here together—"

"You aren't going to see me again, are you?"

"Perhaps not!"

"But you said—you said that time we were together at Farraway that if ever I needed you, wherever I was you would come to me."

"I remember."

"And I *do* need you. Angus, I need your help terribly! You see—Johnnie is trying to make the family believe that I'm unbalanced—that I'm doing terrible things—even that I—*I* tried to kill Uncle Luke last night."

"Good God!"

"He's hinting, he's building up a case against me, Angus," she cried. "He seizes on anything strange that happens in the house and pins it, by suggestion, on to me. I don't know why except that I think it must be that he wants to get rid of me—but he wants *me* to be the whipping boy! Uncle Luke is very, narrow; he'd never forgive Johnnie if *he* left me; or made me so unhappy that *I* left him. So, I'm to be blackened in order that Johnnie will get sympathy, and I shall be the one to be censured." She stopped, took a long, shuddering breath, and looked at Angus. "There's a lot of money at stake. He doesn't want to do anything that will jeopardize that!" She broke off as she saw Angus' eyes, turned to her, darken in sudden horror.

"Great heavens, what's the matter with me?" he cried violently.

"With *you?* What do you mean?"

"That I could be so blind!" Despair replaced violence in his voice. "I thought I was doing the best thing for you; now I know I can't leave you to this danger!"

"I can't face much more! I'm not mad—I never was! But if Johnnie goes on in this way, what is to become of me? Can people be sent mad?"

"Not *you;* not in a thousand years, Tess, my darling!"

"And you'll—come sometimes to see us, Angus, so that I can feel there's someone—"

He turned his head sharply.

"If I can get you a seat on a plane would you return to England?"

"When?"

"As soon as possible—"

"But—"

"For the love of heaven," he cried in sudden exasperation, "if you're going to quibble about money."

She said weakly, "I wasn't. But Johnnie would never let me go."

"Then you must manage to get away without him knowing, even if it means leaving most of your clothes behind. Have you got anyone to go to in England?"

"I have friends who'd put me up until I got a job."

"Then I'll go along to the airline offices today."

"Why do you want me to leave Canada so soon?"

"Because you've made it obvious to me that you're in danger—"

"But Angus—if I leave Canada it means—I won't see you—ever again—?" She tried in vain to keep the despair out of her voice.

"We can't see the future at the moment, Tess—" He turned and took her face in his hands. "Darling, don't misunderstand me! I don't want to lose sight of you—I love you; I want you with me—but there are things you don't understand and I can't explain; I daren't! Only, I know this, I want you out of the way of all that might happen."

"If you love me, you can trust me—tell me—"

"Trust you, yes! But not tell you! Tess, don't question me—let me do what I have to *my* way and then afterwards we can perhaps see more clearly ahead of us." He kissed her mouth, and her eyes closed. "Oh, Tess, I was going to shirk my responsibilities, but now I know I can't! God knows I dread what I have to do, but at least I must see that you are out of the way first."

As he took his hands away from her face she reached out and clung to them.

"Angus, what are you going to do? It's like some—" She sought for the word. "Some macabre riddle—"

"I wish to heaven that were all it is! Tess, be ready to leave at very little notice. Just pack a case you can carry easily. I'll arrange to take you to the airport—"

"How *can* I—"

He ignored her bewildered protest.

"I'll be around to do some more work in the library and I'll give you date and time then.

237

All you will have to do is manage to get out of the house without being stopped."

"I want to sell some jewelry—" she began.

He said earnestly, "You must stop being proud about money! Believe me, this is a very serious matter. I will arrange everything. And now, we must go back." He restarted the car and, letting the engine tick over for a moment, kissed her. "There may never be another chance," he said gravely. "God knows, perhaps in the end it will be I whom you will never forgive!"

He let in the clutch, accelerated and the car purred away, joining the stream of traffic along the highway.

Angus drove fast and in silence. Glancing at him, Tess wondered at the thoughts that gave anger and gravity to his profile.

That he loved her should have brought her joy, should have meant that in spite of all her fear, her heart should have had wings. Instead, it was a paradox—she was loved by the man she wanted to love her, and yet there was no promise that when she left Canada she would ever see him again. True he had said, *"If ever you need me, I will come to you."* Yet what was it, after all, but a promise to come to her aid, to help her or advise her, and then go away again? And even now, in spite of his love for her, what had he told her of himself; what did she know of him save that he was her only friend here and circumstances should warn her not to trust him?

All the excitement, the romantic promise for the future that had surrounded her like sunlight when she had first known Johnnie, was absent with Angus. He had kissed her; he had given her one wonderful morning walking in the sunny woods at Farraway, but he had withheld himself, the essential Angus. He remained unknown, a stranger, a paradox. She wondered, now, if she would ever know more of him than this. And when she reached England, would she be gradually wiped out of his memory? The thought shook her so that she asked herself, in despair, how she was going to bear it since what she felt for him was forever.

"You're cold," Angus said. "You're shivering."

"I'm not acclimatized yet to Canadian winter."

"The car heater's on." He took her hand, eyes still on the road. "Psychological atmosphere can make you as cold as climatic. I wish I could help you; I wish I could hold you close and warm you."

"Instead of which you're sending me away." She heard her own voice, small and as forlorn as a child's.

"To save you from danger, Tess! Because I'm a practical man and sometimes deeds, however cruel they seem, are kinder than all the beautiful words in the world."

How could he love her and yet send her away—so far, that they might never meet again? What was it so on his mind that he wanted her to leave Canada? What strange nightmare was it that was impelling them on, blindly, into an unknown future?

XVII

WHEN HE SET her down at the corner of the road, he took her hand.

"I shall be along one morning soon, Tess, and I shall have everything arranged for you."

"It doesn't seem possible that I shall go away, leaving most of my possessions here—"

"You'll get them, eventually. And if you don't, just look on it as a bargain price to pay for your peace of mind."

"I know—perhaps one values possessions too highly."

"I think we do. Only those who have lost everything really learn that, in the final analysis, nothing is important save health, and peace of mind."

A shadow was cast across the windows of the car. A voice called: "Well! Well!" and Olivia's dark, beautiful face regarded them from above the soft fur collar. Her mouth was amused, her eyes watchful.

Angus wound down the window.

"Hallo," he said lightly. "I thought you worked downtown."

"I do, but I left the manuscript of a beauty article and some photographs behind this morning and so I thought I'd come back to fetch them and have lunch at home. Are you coming in to lunch, Tess, or are you and Angus—"

"We met," he said quickly, "and I offered to run Tess home."

Olivia's eyes measured the length of the road to the house in one meaningful glance. It was as though she said: *But you took good care not to be seen by anyone at home! I wonder what you're up to?*

Tess said quickly: "Thank you, Angus, for the lift. We'll be seeing you?"

"Sure."

"Come and look in on Uncle Luke—" Olivia said.

"I will when he's better. But he won't want a stranger around while he's in bed."

"Oh, he'll be up in a day or so! I know Uncle Luke—"

Tess felt Angus stiffen.

"Keep him in bed!" His voice was sharp with authority. "Keep him safe in bed at least over the weekend."

"If he wants to get up, nobody can stop him! Not even you, *Doctor* Dalzell!" Olivia's voice mocked.

As she turned the handle of the car door, Tess heard Angus urge in a whisper, "Make him stay where he is, Tess!"

"Olivia's right! It's probably impossible unless we tie him to the bed!" She turned to smile at Angus and saw his face, taut with alarm.

"Why keep him in bed? The wound he had was only superficial, and his heart is sound—" she began.

But Angus didn't answer; he scarcely said, "Goodbye," to them as Tess joined Olivia, hunching herself up in her coat.

As they began walking, the car accelerated and passed them, but Angus neither waved nor looked their way.

"What's on *his* mind?" Olivia demanded.

"How should I know?"

"Or perhaps I can guess!" She turned her face towards Tess as they walked along the street under the bare trees. "Perhaps he wants us to keep Uncle Luke in bed because he wants the library to himself for a few more days. How do we know that there aren't some very rare and valuable books among that collection of Uncle Luke's and then, by the time he is well again, Angus Dalzell may have vanished, and none of us will ever see him again! And certain valuable possessions of Uncle Luke will have gone with him!"

"You're quite wrong!"

"How do *you* know, Tess dear?" Olivia asked softly. "How can you be so certain he's no thief? After all, we've proved he's an impostor!"

"No one has proved anything," she burst out loudly. "I won't believe—"

"All right!" Olivia cut in. "Don't get so worked up about it! Carry the torch for him, dear, but don't blame anyone else if you get badly burned!"

They had reached the house and Tess turned in at the gate, aware that her fingers, feeling for her key, were trembling.

Olivia made no attempt to look for hers and her eyes watched Tess' furious thrust at the keyhole. The door opened and Tess walked in, crossed the hall and ran up the stairs without looking back.

She did not expect Johnnie to be home at lunchtime, on a weekday and pushed open their bedroom door and burst in.

Tall and straight as a dart, he swung around from the window as she pulled up with a startled exclamation. Not only was she surprised to find him there, but she had a sudden suspicion that from this window he could see down the road as far as the corner where Angus had stopped the car.

"What's the matter?" He moved from the window towards her. "You look as though I'm an interloper! I assure you I'm not, my dear!"

"I didn't expect you to be home at this time of day, that's all."

"A job I had to do was completed this morning—I sold a house that had been on the market too long, according to Uncle Luke who was asking the earth for it. I came home to get a pat for being a good dog from the master! Where did you and Olivia meet up?"

"At the top of the road."

"You looked good together walking down the road—I'm proud of my two lovely women—" he laughed. "My chestnut wife"—he whipped off her hat and ruffled her hair—"and my raven witch-cousin!"

Would Olivia tell that she had met her with Angus? Tess decided to leave it and see.

She went to the built-in wardrobe and took off her coat. Lights came on as she opened the doors and lit up the colorful row of her clothes. She liked most things she had bought and she faced the fact that she might have to leave them behind her and never see them again. The full realization of what Angus had said rushed over her.

A man she loved against all reason was buying her an air ticket back to England; was, in fact, hurrying her away, urging secrecy. . . . She had already planned to go and the secrecy was necessary if she were ever to be free of Johnnie, but what was so startling was Angus' swift reaction when she told him about Johnnie's behavior towards her, as though she had enabled him to fit a puzzling piece of jigsaw into place.

She closed the closet door and turned. Johnnie was at the mirror brushing his hair.

"If you've been shopping, where are your parcels?"

"I haven't been shopping—"

"Where did you go?"

"Just out—"

He laid down his brush and turned.

" 'Just out'?" He snapped his fingers. "Where? Uptown—downtown?"

She said. "Round the streets. After all, I must get some fresh air. I can't stay in all day—"

"And I never take you out anywhere."

It struck her that, unlike the old happy days in England, here in Canada he had taken her nowhere.

"Well, we're not exactly madly gay in the evenings, are we?" she asked lightly.

"We will be, one of these days. At the moment I've got a lot on my mind."

"Yes, Johnnie, I think you have."

He pivoted around. "What's the subtle inference behind *that?*"

She was at the door. She said as she went through it: "You know your problems, Johnnie! I don't, because you never tell me. You never have been one to share your thoughts—ever—!"

A voice roared down the long, light passage. "That you, Tess?"

"Yes, Uncle Luke," She paused outside his door.

"Come in, come in! Don't hover! I'm not going to eat you!"

He wore a purple dressing gown and the bandage was very white against his russet skin. He looked, sitting up in the great bed, like an old-time Caliph of Baghdad who had taken off his jewels for the night.

"Well, girl," he said before she could ask him how he was, "and how're you getting on?"

"I could do with some more work, Uncle Luke." She deliberately misunderstood him and perching on the arm of a chair smiled serenely at him across the room.

"I'll find you some tomorrow—I'll be up and about again in the morning."

"That you won't!" came Ginevra's rasping old voice.

Tess started and turned as she came, dressed in red with diamonds on her fingers, through the door of his dressing room.

Luke glowered at her.

"What are you doing here?"

"Looking through your clothes—you treat that wardrobe of yours like a rag-bag."

"Doors to the right of me, doors to the left," he grumbled. "That one leading from the dressing-room to the corridor should be locked!"

"Well, it wasn't!" Ginevra snapped. "And, by the way, if you talk about getting up to-morrow, I'll see to it that both your doors are locked—with you inside."

Tess' eyes flew to the dressing-room. The outside door was open and she could see the key in the lock. But there had been no keys in any of the doors a few nights ago. Someone, anticipating that she would try to lock herself in two nights ago, had removed them and had now put them back. She knew, of course, who had done it.

"You'd better go down, Tess. Lunch is on

the table."

She kissed the old man's dry cheek and left him to quarrel happily with Ginevra.

Lunch was not on the table. Walking lightly, Tess pushed open the living-room door. Olivia and Johnnie were sitting side-by-side on the settee and from their faint, furtive movement, she was quite certain that they had been much closer to each other before she startled them.

A thought struck Tess that Olivia could already have told Johnnie that she had met her in Angus' car. But for her own reasons, suspect as they were because she would enjoy stirring up trouble, she had obviously kept quiet and Johnnie had not seen from the bedroom window Angus' car stop at the top of the road. It was like a reprieve after the first flood of fear when she saw Olivia at the car window and guessed at another scene with Johnnie as a result. Yet she knew that the reprieve was only temporary. In her own good time, Olivia would let slip a few casual words, and the whole household would know that she had been with Angus that morning. . . .

XVIII

ON THE FOLLOWING afternoon, when she went to see Uncle Luke, he was puzzled by Angus' non-appearance. "Fine thing, leaving a job half-done!" he complained. "What's the matter with him?"

"I don't know any more than you do, Uncle Luke!"

"When's he coming to get on with cataloguing my books?"

She shook her head helplessly.

"This goddurned doctor of mine!" he went on. "Keeping a man lying around when he's got a heck of a lot to do!"

"You had a nasty hit over the head—"

"I've had more than that in my life, girl, and I haven't been cosseted like some damned silkworm in a cocoon!"

At half-past five they were all assembled in the living-room. Conversation was an effort.

Olivia looked sulky and bored, Johnnie fidgeted with the television until Ginevra snapped at him to get them all some drinks and leave the thing alone.

They heard the doorbell ring and Johnnie said, "Could it be the doctor?"

"He came this morning, had a violent row with Luke and left telling me that if he didn't admire him so, he'd refuse ever to see him again!"

"It may be the Mountjoys for me—" Olivia began, and went to the living-room door. "They said they'd call and pick me up if they were going to the Club."

She broke off as someone opened the door and walked past her into the room without excuse, without invitation. They caught a brief glimpse of Madrigal's startled face, then the living-room door closed.

"Good evening," said Angus Dalzell.

Olivia stiffened. "Good evening, *Mr.* Dalzell. Were you invited?"

"No. I came to inquire how your uncle was."

"He's very much better, *Mr.* Dalzell!"

"You're rather stressing the prefix, aren't you?"

"To try to impress it on you that we know now you're not a doctor." She turned, her eyes full of shining malice. "But our little Tess knew it all along!"

Johnnie moved forward, handsome and smiling and intentionally menacing. "Now that you've heard that Uncle Luke is better, perhaps you've some pressing engagement tonight?"

"You're right, I have!"

"Then—"

"With your uncle—"

"Any date you may have had with him is canceled," Olivia said. "You should have known that after the other night!"

"But we were talking on the telephone this morning. That's why I've called."

"Well, Uncle Luke isn't here, so perhaps you'll come another time."

"Sorry, that's impossible."

The atmosphere of the room was electric with enmity.

"Look, Dalzell—" Johnnie approached him. "We've had a bad accident in this house and Uncle Luke has to be kept quiet. We'd like you to go—or—if you won't, we, may have to seem rather rude."

Angus stood his ground.

"As Mr. Bellairs is expecting me, I don't think that would be expedient."

They heard a sound outside and Ginevra

jumped up.

"It's Luke!"

She was obviously right! Everyone else in that house could walk soundlessly down the stairs. Uncle Luke moved as though he were imitating a tank.

Tess glanced around the room. It was, she thought, like the opening scene of a play—everyone in position; everyone waiting for the leading character to make his entrance. . . .

The door flew open.

"Well, folks?" said Uncle Luke. The bandage had fallen again a little over one eye, his tie was halfway to his ears. But his eyes were bright and he was enjoying himself.

"Of all the crazy, obstinate old men!" Ginevra cried. "You were hit over the head and—"

"And I've got a cut and a bump. What the heck? I'm not dead! Hallo, Dalzell—I thought I heard you arrive."

"How come you dressed and got down so soon?" Ginevra demanded. "Ten minutes ago you were in bed."

"I got dressed hours ago. Everything was underneath my dressing gown." He grinned like a small boy who has outwitted his superiors. "Sit down, sit down everyone. Johnnie, drinks!"

"Oh no, you don't, Uncle Luke! No drink for a long time, doctor's orders!"

"Look, if I want a drink in my own house, I'll blooming well have it—"

"If you so much as touch that tray of drinks, I'll break all the bottles, one by one!" Ginevra threatened. "For heaven's sake, what a man! I'll get you an orange juice."

His face was a study of disgust. He glowered across the room at Olivia. "What are you looking so smug about girl?"

"Thoughts!"

"Out with them."

"Not now, Uncle Luke. Later, when you're better."

"I'll tell you when you can treat me like an invalid. Until then, when I ask a question, answer it!"

Olivia was nothing if not courageous. She lifted her head, her eyes flashed golden; her full red lips were hard and determined.

"Very well! You may as well know, Uncle Luke, that Angus Dalzell has no right to the prefix 'Doctor,' and using it, as he does, is, I believe, an offense in law, or whatever the term is."

"I'm afraid you're mistaken," Angus said very quietly.

"I took the trouble to find out." The angle

of her lovely head was defiant. "So it's pointless to try and bluff. Your name is not on the medical register in Vancouver."

Angus very nearly smiled.

"And you needn't look so damned complacent about it," Johnnie burst out. "We *know!* We *know* you're an impostor, and we're beginning to guess why you're here!"

"Not," said Angus, still speaking quietly, "in a thousand years!"

"Suppose we tell you what we suspect—and we are all—except, of course, Tess, whose judgment doesn't count, poor sweet!—agreed upon it! You think you're clever; you think you've got everything nicely tied up for yourself! You probably expect to be safely in the States before the police can get you. But you won't." Johnnie had moved between Angus and the door. "Now, Dalzell, *let's have the truth!*"

Tess hadn't taken her eyes from Angus' face. Her whole being was alive with her love and fear for him. This was the showdown! Women loved thieves and rogues and vagabonds. She loved an impostor. . . . After tonight she would see to it that they never met again—but it would take a long time for the love in her heart to die . . . and the pain; all the pain of his humiliation tonight to be lived through. . . .

"Since you want the truth," Angus addressed Johnnie, "shall we start at the beginning. Or no, we'll start with the vase—"

"The vase?" Olivia cried, "the *famille noire?*"

Angus turned to Luke. "Have you looked at it lately?"

"Sure, I often look at it—" His eyes were narrowed and alert. He reached up a hand and tipped the bandage a little out of his eye.

"And you're certain that it is genuine?"

"What the devil do you mean?"

"Just that either you were sold a very fine copy, or someone at some time has stolen your original—"

Luke was out of his chair.

Ginevra was crying: "Luke, keep quiet! You know what the doctor said—"

She might have been voiceless and invisible.

"Come on, all of you!" Luke roared and charged across the hall.

He took the keys from his pocket, unlocked the glass case and lifted the great, beautiful vase out.

"Didn't you notice when you bought it that the white had a grayish tinge?"

"I said it looked a bit dirty and they told me that was the color of all genuine *famille noire!*"

"Then look at this one," Angus said. "Look at it, Mr. Bellairs! The white is very pure in

color. This was made by a French firm probably sixty years ago. A fine copy, and certainly
not intended for fraud—but well, someone
has used it, in this instance, for just that!"

Luke looked up and around at them, mo-
mentarily nonplussed—then he lifted the vase
as though he were going to dash it across the
room, changed his mind and set it down on
the table, staring at it.

"Great suffering snakes! I've been robbed."

"I could hazard a guess that it happened the
night Tess arrived and we both heard
someone in the house."

"The key to that glass case is on my key
ring. It's heavy and when I'm playing in
matches, I take it out of my trouser pocket
and leave it, together with odd change, dimes
and quarters, in my coat pocket."

"And your coat was in the dressing room at
the Club?"

"Yes. I changed that night into the jacket I
always wear for curling—"

"So someone could have taken your keys?"

"If you think any member of my Club is a
thief—"

"I'm hazarding a guess. When else do you
leave your key ring behind?"

"Never!"

"So, if you're certain this is not the vase you

yourself bought—"

"Good grief! Do you think Anders and Vinton of New York would risk their reputation by selling me a copy for an original— why, they've got an international name!"

"Then we rule them out and must assume—" Angus began.

"Mr. Dalzell is changing his profession," Olivia broke in, her voice rang with mockery. "He'd have us now believe that he's a detective!"

"Before he changed the conversation"— Johnnie joined the attack—"Dalzell is well aware that I was going to tell you that Olivia is quite right, he's not what he'd like us to think! There is no Dr. Angus Dalzell of Vancouver!" he stopped and waited, his eyes bright with triumph.

Luke's every mood was transparent. He was ready to hit the ceiling.

But Angus spoke first.

"As I've told you, I am a doctor, and I am eventually taking up a post in a Vancouver hospital."

"It's all lies, you know—" Olivia said. "Uncle Luke, he got himself invited into this house under false pretenses."

"The devil, he did! Well?" Uncle Luke glared at him. "Well? Did you deliberately get yourself invited into my house?"

"I did!"

Angus looked at Tess. His eyes said: "Forgive me. Forgive me!"

"And under false pretenses?" Luke shouted.

There came a sound like a drawn breath or triumph from someone in the room—Johnnie or Olivia. . . .

"Then, who are you? And why this playacting?" the old man demanded.

Angus turned to Johnnie.

"I think first you should tell everyone here who you are! Or shall I tell them for you?"

"He's not only an impostor!" Johnnie derided, "he's also mad!"

Angus didn't take his eyes from Johnnie's face. He asked very quietly:

"Did you find it very difficult, at first, answering to an entirely strange name?"

Everyone's gaze moved from Angus' quietly dominating figure to Johnnie. His light blue eyes wavered and flashed. Then he began to laugh softly.

"Sorry I can't answer that question because I don't know what you mean. My name is Johnnie—John, if you want to be formal—Bellairs. And if you want me to prove it—"

"I've no doubt you can! You have all the ev-

idence, haven't you—*except one vital piece*—"
He paused.

Johnnie said in a thin, high voice: "Well, go
on! This is interesting!"

"The vital piece being that you haven't any
diploma to prove that you took your finals in
medicine, have you—"

"Because I never *was* a doctor—"

"But John Bellairs qualified at McGill University in Montreal!"

Johnnie's head shot up, with an unconscious primitive gesture of danger.

"Upstairs, somewhere in your room,"
Angus said, "you have papers proving you are
John Bellairs—papers you stole from the real
owner of that name."

Tess' eyes flashed to Ginevra. She sat huddled and old, gazing, unblinking, at the two
men. Olivia's head was turned to Johnnie;
Luke shot up out of his chair.

"When you've all finished talking in riddles, perhaps I may know what the heck it's
all about?"

Angus ignored him. He was watching
Johnnie.

"Whatever papers of seeming identification
you have, I'm afraid will no longer serve you."

"Proof remains proof!" Johnnie mocked.

"Not when it's stolen—"

"Who *are* you? Some blamed busy-body? Well, get out of this house! Get out!"

"Maybe I will when I have formally introduced you to everyone here—*Peter Lagarde!*"

Tess caught her breath sharply: her hands flew to, her face. "But that's—Johnnie's half-brother—"

"That's right," said Angus. "You're looking at John Bellairs' half-brother, a man with no claim to relationship with this family."

Johnnie made a movement as though coiling up within himself; rapier-slim, head alerted, ready to strike.

"If you don't get out in one second, Dalzell, I'll throw you out, and I won't make a gentle job of it!"

"You were always violent—that's what got you your jail sentence."

The door was jerked open. Johnnie's arm flailed. Olivia was across the room in a flash of fury and triumph. If Johnnie could be proved an imposter, the whole beautiful fortune was hers! Somehow, Angus was managing to stave off Johnnie's attack.

Ginevra cried: "Luke, do something, for heaven's sake. Ask where John Bellairs is—ask—how you can find him and prove—"

"Dalzell—" Luke roared, "where is my nephew? Is he alive?"

"I am John Bellairs," said Angus.

The room rocked for Tess. She heard Olivia's hard forced laugh. "Another impostor, Uncle Luke! Shall I call the police?"

"But he died!" Johnnie hissed. "He died in a train crash out in Bolivia!" Hate rasped his voice. But there was also triumph, as though in his own defeat, he would also drag Angus— "I have a newspaper cutting to prove it!"

"My name was given as among the dead. But I lived. There was too much confusion at the time for accuracy. I was taken to a hospital, and I recovered."

"Prove it! But you can't, can you? You haven't any papers to show you're John Bellairs!"

"Because you stole them!"

Johnnie was framed in the doorway. His blue eyes blazed at them.

"Think up a better story, Dalzell!"

"You went to my apartment when you read that I was dead; you stole my identification papers, and then you set fire to the room. It can all be proved, Lagarde—every single accusation I make!"

There was a movement at the door and the next moment Johnnie wasn't there.

Luke brushed his hand across his eyes. "So I've been fooled!" For the first time he sounded shaken and old. Then his spirit rallied.

"Well, what are you standing about for? Get after him!"

Angus said quietly, "Wait!"

"For that impostor to get away? Not on your life!"

"You'd probably like to see proof that *I* am John Bellairs."

"The proof is in Lagarde's escape." He tried to push past Angus at the door.

"It's all right, he won't get away!" He glanced at the clock. "Give him two minutes' start—"

"To get where? Over the border?"

"No. To go where I believe he has hidden the K'ang Hsi, vase. If you want it back, do as I say. I've a very fast car, I'll catch him up! If we go too soon and he knows we're following him, he'll lead us away from the place I believe he's heading for and then we'll never be able to check on anything."

"You mean *he* stole the vase?"

"I believe so. He was the only one who could have had access to the keys in your coat pocket."

Olivia cried: "On the night of the curling competition at the Club, he went out to get cigarettes just before the end of the match. He was gone a long time—"

Angus turned to Luke. "That was the night Tess arrived. He could go to your coat to fetch something without being questioned, because he was accepted as your nephew. That's why he didn't meet you at the station, Tess. I don't believe he even intended to. He had to replace the vase when the house was empty, and I believe you said that rarely happened. He had to exchange those vases before Tess arrived and that night, when you were all out, was his last chance—at least that's how I see it!"

"He probably saw a copy of a *famille noire* when he went down to New York," Olivia said, "and that gave him the idea."

Ginevra was leaning against the desk, her arms crossed tightly across her thin, bent body.

"It was there"—she rocked backwards and forwards—"in his face, only you didn't see it. It was in the mask; the dark, secret, lying side of him! That's why he destroyed it!"

Suddenly Angus moved. "I'm going after him now."

"You've given him too long a start."

"Didn't you hear? He had trouble starting up his car. As I told you, if we'd tried to hold him, we'd have found nothing. We had to let him go and to let him think we weren't after him."

"Suppose he's not going for the vase—"

"It's a chance we must take! He's obviously after something—" Angus was across the hall, Luke and Tess following.

Olivia called: "And after this, you've got to prove *your*self Mr. Dalzell—"

"He will!" Ginevra said. "He will!"

Angus glanced over his shoulder.

"Stay here, Tess, do you hear?"

"I'm coming with you—"

"I won't harm him, if that's what you're afraid of!"

"But *he* might harm *you!*"

"Out of my way, girl!" Luke charged, almost pushing her over. "My coat—get it, Tess—in the cloakroom there—"

Ginevra cried: "Stay, Luke! Let Angus go!"

The inner door opened and then the outer. Luke snatched his coat from Tess, dragging it on as he went. An icy draught whirled around them. Angus was at his car. Luke after him.

"I could almost pity you, Tess." Olivia's voice was soft, "Married to an impostor. And he nearly got away with it!"

But Tess seized the handle of the car door and dragged at it. Angus was revving the engine.

"Get back, girl." Luke had a hat perched rakishly above the bandage around his head.

Ginevra called in her strange, rasping voice that the wind caught and turned into a husky scream: "You're mad, Luke—going out in this—"

No one took any notice. Tess almost fell in as the car shot forward.

Angus said without turning around; "If we meet any traffic lights at 'Stop,' Uncle Luke, will you get Tess out of this car? I don't care if she has to walk back!"

"This is my problem as much as anyone's!" She sat on the edge of the seat, swaying to the motion and speed of the car.

"Where are we going?" Luke asked from the seat next to Angus.

"Chillawoka."

"Lord's sake, why?"

"Peter is a stranger here, so he would have no friends he could trust sufficiently to plant a small crate on. People would ask questions! But he'd have to get that vase out of the house and he daren't sell it here in Toronto. I think as he goes so often to Chillawoka, he saw your cottage there as a temporary hiding-place. When he knew tonight that he couldn't bluff any longer, he was determined that he'd salvage one thing from the wreck I'd made of his plans. Are you all right, Uncle Luke?"

"Of course I'm all right—"

"I had to let you come because I don't know just where your summer cottage is. You must guide me when we get near to the Lake."

"It's only just off the road. But suppose he hasn't gone there—suppose he's gone the other way, towards Buffalo?"

"He'd never get the vase through the Customs at the frontier—or himself. If, when we get to the cottage, he isn't there I'm going to get in touch with the police and give them the number of his car and a description of him. They'll contact the Customs men. We've got plenty of time for that—he can't possibly be at Buffalo for hours yet. If he makes for Montreal and a ship, then we've got time to stop him there, too. But my guess is Chillawoka."

"With a good start—"

"The ignition of his car delayed him, he'll be only just ahead of us." The Chrysler snaked through the traffic, Luke fretting at every forced stop.

Once Angus said, "Tess, please get out at the next lights, and no arguing—I can't stop long enough for that! This isn't something for you to be involved in."

"You seem to forget that I'm involved more than anyone!" she said shakenly.

Angus was silent, but the car was slowing down.

"You'd better do what Angus says," Luke cautioned. "This isn't a job for a woman."

"But I can't go back and just sit waiting!" she protested. "Uncle Luke, you must understand that!"

Angus was pulling the car into the side of the road.

"The lights are green," she said desperately. "Angus, don't stop; it's no use, because I won't get out! I've *got* to come with you!"

"He may be dangerous! We don't even know whether he's not armed! God knows what he'll do when we catch him up! And you being with us won't help, girl!"

"I can't help that, I've got to come. Go on!" she urged as the car stopped. "Angus, you're wasting time! *Get on;* because I won't get out whatever you try to do."

Something in her tone and her despairing repetition must have registered her resolution to see this thing through, terrible though it might be. She heard Angus murmur. "All right." Then he accelerated, moving away again into the stream of traffic. He drove with the swift, deadly accuracy of judgment of a police car, she thought watching him.

"We've lost him!" Luke said.

"If he's going where I think he is, we'll pick him up soon."

Tess sat back and drew a breath of relief. It was easier—though they could not understand—to be active, to be with them, watching everything that happened, rather than wait in doubt and anxiety at home.

They're chasing Johnnie as though he's a criminal . . . and Johnnie is my husband. Johnnie, who is a criminal. . . .

Tess felt her eyes stiff with staring ahead down the light-dazzled road; headlamps glaring, overhead lights pouring down on to the wide ribbon of the road. All this tension, this activity—and yet her mind was not able to take its full impact. . . .

XIX

PRESENTLY THEY hit the highway and Angus trod hard down on the accelerator. Sixty, seventy, eighty. . . .

"Johnnie—we'll go on calling him Johnnie—" Angus said, "never dreamed when he bought a white car that he'd regret it! It'll be conspicuous along this lighted highway." He leaned a little over the wheel, peering ahead.

"Look, there it is! I don't want to get too near, so watch, please, in case I miss where he turns off—"

"It'ud have to be at the Chad Valley Garage—" Luke said. "Then on to Meynell Heights. After that it's a straight road."

Angus' hands were steady on the wheel. Tess sat tense and watching, just able to see the rear light of a car which, as it passed under the great highway lights, shone white.

In that car is a man I knew as Johnnie Bel-

lairs, a man I married under that name. . . .

Johnnie Bellairs—heir to half a fortune. . . .

Luke was asking: "You may as well tell us as we're going along, how all this happened."

"You and my father lost touch with each other after you went out East for the first time—"

"I was eighteen and he was just a kid—there was twelve years difference between us: I heard years later that your father had married and left England for South America to some job he had offered him in Buenos Aires. Go on from there."

"My father died and my mother married again. Peter was the son of that marriage. I was sent up to McGill University in Montreal and I lost sight of him—I heard he'd broken away from home after some trouble over a forged check. Soon after I passed my finals my mother died and I went to Bolivia to work for a while in a medical research station there. When I finished, I decided to go up to Lima. The Peruvians were doing work up there that interested me. I kept my apartment on in La Paz because I only expected to be away a few weeks. Then I was coming back to pack up and leave for Vancouver and a job there. On the morning I was to leave for Lima, Peter telephoned. He had arrived, he said, from

271

Montevideo. It was my first contact with him for fifteen years."

"But if he came to see you, then you'd have recognized him here—"

"I had no time to see him. I asked for his address but he said he'd call me again when I got back from Lima. I caught that train. Fifty miles on, it jumped the rails and crashed. There was a heavy death toll and dreadful confusion because the place was so isolated. My name was among the dead. But I was taken to a hospital and I recovered. When I was well enough, the news was broken to me that my apartment in La Paz had been badly damaged by fire. All my private papers had been lost. Of course, I went to Buenos Aires where I got new identification papers. The whole thing took a long time. I asked my stepfather about Peter—he had neither seen nor heard of him for years."

The car leapt along the wide road.

Tess sat forward, her back aching, desperate to hear everything, to learn painfully that she had married a man she had never really known.

"When I eventually reached Vancouver, I was told I wasn't in a fit state to start work straight away. They suggested I should have a long break. Doing nothing never amuses me, so I became ship's doctor and traveled, as you know. When I arrived in Vancouver, fit again and ready to take up my medical post, I saw in a newspaper that you had been searching for a nephew and had found him. It gave his name—John Bellairs. But I was John Bellairs and I seemed to remember my father talking about a brother of his he'd lost touch with who was living in Toronto. So I came to see what this man was like who had taken my name. It dawned on me that it could be Peter—and that he could have stolen my identification papers in La Paz. That, with his tarnished reputation, he might have seen this as a way to start a new life. He might even have remembered that I had a rich uncle on my father's side. I don't know—I can only guess. All I do know is that he must have set fire to my apartment to give the impression the papers of identity were burned. And then his chance came when you found him in England."

"We were British," Luke said, "that's why I had a feeling my nephew might have returned to England. Canada was the last place I thought of looking—"

"You wouldn't have found me here, anyway. At the time you were looking for me, I was footloose in the East, in between working as ship's doctor. I hadn't begun my life in Vancouver."

"The car's disappeared!" Tess cried.

"It must have turned down towards Meynell Heights; that's the Chillawoka road."

"Then we're all right."

"Funny thing," Luke commented, "your meeting Tess on the train!"

"She was apparently your niece by marriage, Uncle Luke, and so the press recorded her arrival in the States. I read, also, that Mrs. John Bellairs was at Sarraway Fields in Connecticut staying with friends before coming to join her husband here. I told you, Tess, that first time we met in the train that as Uncle Luke's niece by marriage you'd be in the gossip columns, that your doings would be news—"

"You said: 'You can't escape, Mrs. Bellairs.' "

(And I couldn't! I can't . . .)

"One man knew the story as far as I knew it at that time," Angus continued. "A colleague of mine in New York. He arranged my introduction as Angus Dalzell to friends of yours in Sarraway Fields."

It was all so neat! Tess thought. *So easy!*

"I traveled to Toronto with you, because I wanted to find out what I could about the man who was impersonating me—I guessed by then who it was. But you gave nothing away—

you couldn't, because you knew nothing!" He steered his car skillfully past two trucks. "The rest you both know. I was going to maneuver a meeting with Uncle Luke somehow—the fact that Johnnie didn't meet you at the station was my piece of luck! I'm sorry, Tess, that sounds ruthless, put that way!"

"It's all right I—I understand!"

"I hope you do!"

She understood all right. She had been used to stalk a criminal! Her husband. . . .

"You knew nothing of all this?" Luke demanded of her.

Angus answered. "Tess knew nothing!"

"I'm sorry, girl! But I'll look after you. I've grown fond of you even though you're no relative by marriage—"

But Tess scarcely heard him. One thing stood out with humiliating clarity. Angus had not been coming to the house because of her! All the things he had said to her and which she had interpreted romantically, daring to believe she had a friend—and more than a friend—in him, had been of her own blind imagining. He had even said that he loved her; but was that, too, part of all the dreadful unreality?

"Slow down here—" Luke said.

A large, illuminated sign at the side of the

road bore the painted words: CHILLAWOKA. DRIVE WITH CARE.

The white car was no longer in sight.

"The cottage is just down that lane."

"Then we'll get out and walk"—Angus slowed down—or rather, *I* will. You two stay here."

Neither took any notice of the order. They got out, not even closing the car doors for fear of making a sound. Carefully they made their way down the short, slippery lane that had been partially cleared of snow. Here and there through the thick trees, the moon gleamed on the snow-covered roofs of the elaborate cottages. And then, in a clearing, they saw a white car with all its lights off.

Angus went up to it and peered in. He turned to Luke.

"The seat has been tipped up in readiness for something: and there's a space under it large enough to hide something in. I make a guess. That's how he was going to get the vase over the frontier. The vase—or whatever it is he's after!"

Luke asked, "Did he own a gun?"

Tess shook her head. "I don't know."

"Oh well, here's going and finding out!" Luke walked ludicrously, like a bear on tiptoe. "And my K'ang Hsi vase is here?"

"We'll have to see," Angus said cautiously.

Nothing in her life, Tess thought, could ever be so bad as this! Johnnie had killed her love and Angus had, in brief and precious moments, brought it to vibrant life again.

But the flowering was only within herself. Angus—he would always be "Angus" to her—had used her to get an entrée into that house; he had had compassion for her, but compassion never became love. . . .

She saw, as she crept shivering along the dark path behind them, how everything he had said to her could be interpreted as sympathy for her position; even his words of love, to inspire her confidence in him!

"Keep back," Angus suddenly said.

They had reached the cottage almost before they realized it.

The door was open and everything was silent. Nothing stirred in that silver and sable world.

"Is there a back door?" Angus asked in a low voice.

"Yes."

"I think he heard us and has gone out that way. Get to his car, Uncle Luke; take the ignition key; immobilize it before he can get to it."

Angus began to run around the side of the cottage; Tess followed. They saw Johnnie for a moment outlined in moonlight, hesitating, listening like a figure carved in ebony. Then, as though he had seen Luke cross the luminous night to his car, Johnnie swung around towards the woods. He was carrying something in his arms and that and the deep snow was impeding, his speed. He stumbled, head forward, like a blind man, and then he became lost in the blackness.

"Stop, you fool!" Angus yelled.

The deep snow muffled the sound of footsteps. Helplessly, they plunged into the gloom after him, their feet sinking into the snow. Then, from behind them, came Luke's voice, splitting the silence with a roar.

"Stop! It's dangerous that way. Angus! Tess! Come back! There's a ravine—you're almost on it—"

Angus flung himself back and put out an arm, Tess crashed into him. She leaned, breathless and off balance, on his protecting arm.

The moon shone on the scene immediately at their feet. A great ravine yawned there, full of silver light and deep, somber shadow. Along its bed was the steel-gray gleam of the frozen river that fed Chillawoka Lake.

"Johnnie!" She heard her own thin scream. *"Johnnie!"*

There was no sound, no movement, no echo.

Angus went cautiously forward, holding on to clumps of bushes with both hands, not daring to trust the soft and deadly snow at the ravine's edge. When he was sure that he still stood where firm ground lay under the packed snow, he leaned forward and shone his torch down. It showed him nothing. He moved cautiously another few inches and then further still.

"The snow will give way!" Tess cried.

But before she had finished speaking Angus had turned. She sensed, rather than saw, the great shiver that went through him. He put out a hand and thrust her back.

"Don't look! Uncle Luke—" He raised his voice.

The old man was coming towards them. "I've immobilized the car—"

"It doesn't matter. It doesn't matter—any—longer—" Angus' hand lay across Tess' shoulder. "He's down there—I could just see him in the moonlight. Where can you go for help?"

"The ranger's hut has a telephone communication with the police. It's just across the track."

"Will you go and get help? And Tess, go back to the cottage. He may have just broken a limb—*go back*, I tell you!" he added, as she hesitated.

Her mind, like her body, was numb. Angus shone his torch on to the path for her as Luke left them for the ranger's hut. She found the path and began to walk, but soon, because her mind wasn't on what she was doing, she found that she had wandered away from the track and was sinking almost knee-deep in the snow. She found her way back only to lose it again, but at last she identified Luke's cottage by the big white car standing near it.

She went through the door into the darkness, turned into the great log-walled living-room and, groping her way to a chair, sat down and closed her eyes.

Time lost meaning for her. Dimly she heard voices, heard a car drive up, saw strong lights flashing through the trees. She remained there, unable to move, unable even to wonder how they would bring Johnnie up from that far, frozen depth.

Her feet were numb. She took her boots off and almost mechanically rubbed the circulation back. Even in such moments of sheer despair, she thought, one fought for survival!

Presently footsteps sounded. How long had passed? Ten minutes? An hour? Two hours? Shivering she looked up as lights switched on and Luke stamped into the room.

"Girl, you'll freeze! Why didn't you turn on the fire?"

"I hadn't got a match."

"It's automatic." He switched it on.

Tess looked at Angus. "Johnnie?"

He said, "Tess, I'm afraid you'd better know straight away. That fall—he couldn't—have survived it!"

She covered her face with her hands.

"Believe me, Tess—I wanted no violence!"

"He made his own violence," said Luke. "God rest his soul!"

"We've got to go and identify him in his real name. But not yet. Take your stockings off, girl, and dry them." He was putting her boots close to the fire. "It'll ruin the leather, but never mind. I'm going to fetch something to warm us up. I keep most things up here—I've always, thought that sometime or other you young people would use this place for weekend winter sports—there's skating and a bit of skiing here." He went out of the room, hat over the bandage around his head, coat collar up, heedless of his soaking trouser-legs, tough as an old warrior.

Tess looked at Angus. "Was he after the vase?"

"It was in the crate he carried. It doesn't exist any more."

So, the things Johnnie had accused Angus of, had been *his* sins!

She sat there, huddled by the fire. Angus brought a cushion and made her put her feet on it.

"All those things that happened!" she said. "Uncle Luke's accident—Johnnie couldn't have done that!"

"You know now why I wanted to get you right away from it all. I saw that if Johnnie became desperate, you would be in danger. I wanted to get you out of the country before the climax would have to come. It would have been easier for you to hear if you were thousands of miles away."

She said again, "Johnnie couldn't have tried to harm Uncle Luke that night, could he?"

"You've had to face so much—face this, Tess, get the whole thing cleared up. It's the only way you can hope to start again!"

"He *did* do it? But—how?"

"I've tried to figure it out," Angus said. "There's a low balcony outside the landing window, just over the back door. I think the mewing of Aunt Ginevra's cat was meant to bring Uncle Luke out into the garden. He might not have come—if he hadn't, I suppose there'd have been other ways. The icicle was incidental. Johnnie was waiting for Uncle

Luke when he came out of the back door and he leaned down and struck him hard with something—heaven knows what! When he saw the broken pieces of ice around he probably guessed we'd come to the conclusion that Uncle Luke slipped and hit his head against the step. When he realized that Aunt Ginevra and I were puzzled about the type of wound, he decided that the safest thing to do was to be suspicious as well. It *could* only be that way, Tess!" he went on gravely.

"I'd been giving Johnnie time to get caught out somehow, but he was too clever and I no longer dared risk waiting any longer. Johnnie was getting impatient for that inheritance—Uncle Luke was too fit, too vigorous! I knew that I'd have to force the whole thing into the open before he was well enough to get around again, or there'd be another accident. And the police would have had to be called in, that was why when Olivia saw us together in the car, and said Uncle Luke would be up and about in a day, I knew I'd got to act at once—I dare not wait any longer."

"Johnnie tried to—to incriminate me—" Tess sat, her hands held out, small and white and frozen, to the heat of the fire.

"I'd begun to realize that, Tess! He had to have a suspect for anything that might happen—"

"Here you are." Luke came back bearing a bottle and glasses. "Brandy!"

"But not for you!" Angus said. "I'm sorry—"

"All right. I'll make myself some black coffee." His rip-roaring self-indulgence seemed to have left him—a man had died and what one drank to combat the penetrating cold in this solemn moment was no longer important. The old giant was bearing up magnificently, but with shock had come a new gentleness.

He looked at Tess. "I didn't mean it to be this way, girl!" he said.

"I know!" She took the glass of brandy he had poured out and set it on a small table. "I'll make coffee for you, Uncle Luke."

"You don't know where everything is. And you can't go walking around in bare feet! Stay where you are."

They were alone again.

"What can I say, Tess. If I hadn't turned up, none of this would have happened."

"So much was lost for me before you came! I wanted to be free of him, but, oh Angus, I—I never wanted him dead!"

She couldn't stop the tears. Angus sat on the arm of her chair and gathered her to him.

"Nobody could have foreseen what happened tonight! Heaven knows, nobody could have wished it! But you know everything now, you've had to face it and it'll be easier to get over it. Life is a cycle and bad times end! Tess—oh Tess—*darling*—"

The word was real. She recognized the place from which it came—not from compassion but from love.

"It may not help you for the moment"—he held her close, speaking with his lips against her throbbing temple—"but one day when all this is over, I shall find you, wherever you are."

Johnnie had said, "I shall never let you go . . ." and it had filled her with fear. Now someone else did not want to let her go—the man called Angus—and she knew that some day, all would be right with her world.

Center Point Publishing
Brooks Road ● PO Box 1
Thorndike ME 04986-0001 USA

**(207) 568-3717
US & Canada:
1 800 929-9108**